I0451539

The Genesis Connection

*The Prequel - A Lucas Forge Novel
Book 0*

By Scott Sindelar

ORIGINALLY PUBLISHED BY:
Clean House Press ISBN 978-1-888774-11-5
ADDITIONAL PUBLICATIONS
Amazon Kindle

1

Special Offer

Get a Free Short Story

The Man Who Would Be Savior

Go to

ScottSindelarBooks.com

Dedication

This book is dedicated to my wife, the fascinating, fetching, and exuberant, Susan Carroll Sindelar. Without her unwavering support and sacrifice, this book would not have been possible.

Chapter 1

The Director

The autumn sun was burning its way through the dense fog, rolling in waves, concealing the browning grass of the Langley facility courtyard. Straining his espresso colored eyes, Anthony Triana was trying to see past the water tower and into the thick primeval forest beyond. Seeing the forest always gave him comfort, allowing him to organize his data cluttered mind. The wooded area served as a soft contrast to the harsh, stark efficiency and florescent lighting inside the government complex.

Placing his hands on the fifth story window frame, Triana leaned forward, his long aquiline nose almost touching the glass. *Come on, dammit. Let me see you*. The fog was fighting valiantly against the sun's penetrating warmth, but soon dissipated enough so that he could see the tops of the tallest trees.

The buzzing of the intercom on his desk ripped him mercilessly from his reverie. *What now?* Pushing away from the window, and turning slowly on his short legs, Triana crossed the thickly carpeted room to his heavy mahogany desk. Pressing the intercom button with his stubby index finger, he answered briskly, "Yes, Cecelia?"

The woman's voice replied with a soft British accent, "Agent Holstein is here to see you for the briefing, sir."

Moving quickly behind his desk, he sat down in his specially designed leather chair that made him appear taller than he was. Opening a file on his desk, he pressed the intercom. "Thank you, Cecelia. Send him in."

The buzzing from the door was followed by a loud click. The door opened, but the frame was darkened by a tall brute of a man in an ill-fitting dark suit. A bulge on his right side betrayed the fact that he was carrying a side arm, poorly concealed by his jacket. Gripping a standard sized briefcase in his meaty left hand, he made it to the front of the desk in three easy strides. Standing at attention, he towered over the desk.

Pretending to look at the file in front of him, Triana did not acknowledge his presence. *That briefcase looks like a child's lunchbox in his massive hand.* He kept the man standing for a full minute before finally saying, "Take a seat, agent Holstein."

Clearing his throat, Holstein replied in an incongruously resonant tenor, "Thank you, sir."

Watching the man sit gingerly in one of the two armless chairs, Triana wondered if it would support the man's bulk. Holstein placed the briefcase atop his thick, muscular thighs and snapped open the locks.

Despite being seated, he still looked down at the man behind the desk.

Triana started, "Well, what do you have for me?"

"There is this new agent, Director. He just completed training at the farm. I've never seen anyone like him. He finished college at 16 with a BS degree in psychology. He finished his PhD in less than three years. We recruited him while he was in grad school, but he insisted on first spending a year with a forensic psychologist, and then two years in special ops and intelligence with the Army. He said it was something about a promise he made to his father. He spent black ops time in Panama as a scout/sniper, before joining us here."

Triana's expression changed only with a slight raising of his eyebrows. Nodding once at Holstein, he said, "Go on."

Removing a thick sheaf of paper from the briefcase, Holstein said, "Here's the kicker, Director. Look at the title of his PhD dissertation."

Leaning forward, Holstein, passed the document toward Director Triana. Staring into Holstein's golden eyes for a few seconds before looking at the document, he let his eyes drift downward to the title page.

Empirical Methods for Criminal Profiling and Interrogation in Counterterrorism.

Holstein continued, "I had a couple of beers with him the other night. I found out that he was invited to teach a course at the Behavioral Analysis Unit-1, the counter-terrorism unit at Quantico, based on his research and on his, um, work in Panama. This guy is wicked smart and was at the top of his class in handgun and rifle marksmanship." Looking down, Holstein shifted in his chair and cleared his throat.

Leaning forward, Triana asked, "But there's something more, isn't there, agent Holstein?"

"Sir, I thought the FBI might try to steal him away, but he told me, and I quote, "I want to cut off the heads of snakes before they get into our country, not after." Sir, I want him on my team."

Leaning back, Triana steepled his fingers in front of his face and stared at Holstein, who appeared to be holding his breath. "What aren't you telling me?"

"Begging your pardon, sir. When he and I were drinking the other night, my plan was to interview him and see what makes him tick, to see if he would be a good fit. Damned if he didn't get me talking, and he got a whole lot more out of me than I got out of him. He's 10 years younger than me. There is only one other man that, uh, that ever did that to me."

"And who was that, Holstein?"

"Sir, it was you, sir."

Director Anthony Triana turned his head to look out the window. The fog had given up, finally revealing his precious forest.

Chapter 2

Three years earlier

"I don't think he did it." Dr. Lucas Forge leaned forward in his chair, placing his hands in his lap. He looked confidently into the eyes of the attorney standing across from him. Inside, he was not feeling as confident as he hoped he looked.

District Attorney Sheila Kurkowski stared back at him, with what she hoped was an intimidating gaze.

"Mr. Forge," she started.

"That's Dr. Forge, counselor," he corrected.

"Ah, yes, Dr. Forge. I still have trouble thinking that someone as young as you, you are barely twenty years old, could be a doctor."

"But you're not a real doctor, are you?" she taunted. "I am sure you have seen the report by the eminent forensic psychiatrist, Dr. David Ford, M.D., who, by the way, has 30 years of experience in forensic psychiatry. In fact, he started his practice before you were even born. Isn't that true?"

Lucas took a breath and let it out slowly. He had been deposed by DA Kurkowski several months ago on a different case. He had made the rookie mistake of underestimating her knowledge and understanding of criminal psychology. He had also not prepared as thoroughly as he should have, and could not quote empirical sources for his conclusions. She tore him up on the witness stand and he left the courtroom feeling embarrassed and ashamed. He learned many valuable lessons that day, and he was determined to be a credible expert for the court in this case.

"I am sorry, counselor, but you asked a compound question, or rather, three questions. Which one do you wish me to answer?"

Glaring at him, she replied, "I want you to answer all of them."

Although he knew the three questions, he was not going to make it easy for her. More importantly, he did not want to confuse the judge. He responded, "Can you repeat the first question, please?"

Looking down at her notes, she began again, "Dr. Forge, you are not a real doctor, are you?"

Lucas took another breath, but before he could answer, the judge interrupted.

"Ms. Kurkowski, you have already stipulated to his credentials and the court accepts his qualifications as an expert witness, and yes, counselor, he is a real doctor. Please move on."

"Yes, your Honor."

Lucas noticed that her hands gripped her notes more tightly.

"Dr. Forge, have you seen the report by Dr. Ford?"

"Yes, I have."

"Isn't it true that the report by Dr. Ford, the medical doctor, came to very different conclusions about the defendant than you did?"

Lucas simply answered, "Yes."

"Isn't it true that Dr. Ford concluded that the defendant was a psychopath?"

"Yes."

"Despite his 30 years of experience as a forensic psychiatrist, you, with less than a year of experience, disagree with his conclusions?"

"Yes."

"Do you disagree with his conclusion that the defendant is also a cocaine addict?"

"Technically, yes."

"Technically, yes? Will you explain to the court why you disagree with this conclusion?

"Yes. The defendant had a two-year history of progressive cocaine abuse and resulting cocaine dependence. After his arrest, he voluntarily admitted himself to a 30-day substance abuse treatment program. This was followed by a three month relapse prevention program and one year of aftercare. During these 15 months, he had random urine drug screens that verified his continued sobriety. I evaluated him during the last month of his recovery treatment program. At that time, he had been clean and sober from cocaine for almost 16 months."

Lucas paused a moment for effect. "The correct diagnosis is Cocaine Dependence, Severe, in sustained remission. The term 'cocaine addict' is not an official diagnosis. It is recognized by neither the American Psychological Association nor the American Psychiatric Association. That is why I disagreed with the pejorative diagnosis made by Dr. Ford."

Lucas noticed that the judge was taking notes, while the DA was grinding her teeth.

Kurkowski continued, "Dr. Forge, in his report, Dr. Ford concluded that the defendant was a severe psychopath and that this was the reason that he murdered his grandmother. We have the evidence that he buried his grandmother in a shallow grave outside of Sedona, Arizona. We have evidence that he stole money from his patients. We have evidence that he lied to cover up his addiction. Are these not the hallmarks of a psychopath?"

Lucas took another breath, gathering his thoughts before answering.

"The diagnosis of 'psychopath' is also not a recognized diagnosis in the current diagnostic manual. The current diagnostic term is Antisocial Personality Disorder, and it includes many criteria that the defendant does not meet. First, the diagnosis requires a previous diagnosis of Conduct Disorder that had to be present prior to the age of 15. The defendant had no criminal history, prior to the age of 15. He had no problems or altercations with authority and he was an exemplary student, both academically and socially. Without this previous diagnosis of Conduct Disorder, one cannot make a diagnosis of Antisocial Personality Disorder as an adult."

Lucas knew he was on solid scientific ground, and wanted the judge to have the correct information. Lucas continued, "The defendant also does not meet several other criteria for Antisocial Personality Disorder. There is no evidence for failure to conform to societal norms, which would include him having previous arrests. He had no previous arrests. There is no evidence for impulsivity or failure to plan ahead. There is no evidence for irritability or aggressiveness. There is no evidence for consistent irresponsibility, or failure to maintain work. I also did not find evidence for reckless disregard for the safety of himself or others. Therefore, he does not meet the criteria for Antisocial Personality Disorder."

"But, Dr. Forge, the defendant admitted that he buried his grandmother in a shallow grave. Isn't that evidence enough to diagnose him as a psychopath?"

"No, it is not."

"On what do you base your conclusions?" she shouted.

Lucas knew that she should not have asked a question for which she did not know the answer. He decided to provide the answer for the court.

"The defendant told me that he was complying with her wish. He said that she told him that she wanted to be buried outside Sedona, near one of her favorite spots."

"So, Dr. Forge, the defendant told you this story, and you believed him?"

Lucas continued, "For me, his story was not enough evidence. I confirmed this evidence when I interviewed his two siblings separately. They both told me that this was their grandmother's wish. They admitted they did not know if it was legal to do this, but they all felt obligated to comply with what she wanted."

"So he illegally buried her after he killed her?"

"It is up to the court to determine whether or not he actually killed his grandmother. It is up to the court to determine whether he had the motive, the intent, and the means. I was unable to determine a motive for him to kill his grandmother. She had no assets and no insurance policy. According to the family, the defendant was taking care of her in his home and was happy to do so. His behaviors, prior to her death, suggested that he loved her. According to the medical examiner's report, she died from a massive heart attack, after a long history of coronary artery disease."

"Are you aware, Dr. Forge, that after she died, he wrapped her body in plastic and left her on her bed for at least two days before stuffing her into a freezer?"

"That is my understanding."

"What kind a person does that, Dr. Forge?"

"The kind of person who thought he was dying."

"Is it not true that the defendant told you this story, that he thought he was dying? How do you know that he wasn't lying to you?"

"I interviewed his physician, Dr. Campbell, who diagnosed him with CMV, cytomegalovirus. It is a common virus that is currently incurable, but in most adults, it is not fatal."

"And yet, the defendant told you he was dying. Is that not correct? So, he was lying to you."

"He believed he was dying," Lucas replied.

"Are you aware, Dr. Forge, that Dr. Campbell testified in court that he never told the defendant that he was dying?"

"Yes, I read Dr. Campbell's medical records."

"So, the defendant concocted this story that he was dying, and you believed him?"

"I also interviewed his dentist, Dr. Matthews. Dr. Matthews had been his dentist since he was a child. According to his curriculum vita, Dr. Matthews specializes in pediatric and child dentistry. He became friends with the defendant and continued to see him as his patient throughout his adulthood."

"What does this dentist have to do with a medical diagnosis?"

"As I noted, Dr. Matthews was a pediatric dentist. In his practice, he previously had two families who lost their babies to CMV. He was under the mistaken impression, therefore, that CMV was a fatal illness. When he learned that the defendant was diagnosed with CMV, he became alarmed, and told the defendant that he better get his affairs in order. Essentially, he told the defendant that he was dying."

"Dr, Campbell testified that he never specifically told the defendant that he was dying. Isn't that correct, Dr. Forge?"

"That is my understanding from Dr. Campbell and his medical records."

"Didn't Dr. Campbell tell you that he corrected the defendant's misunderstanding? Dr. Campbell told the defendant that he was not dying."

"That is correct. The defendant, however, did not believe Dr. Campbell at that point. In his cocaine-induced paranoia, he thought Dr. Campbell was lying to him and the defendant never went back to Dr. Campbell."

"And again, Dr. Forge, that is what the defendant told you?"

"Yes. According to the medical records, Dr. Campbell never saw the defendant again after that appointment. In my interview with the dentist, Dr. Matthews, he told me that he had two subsequent telephone conversations with the defendant. Both phone calls were initiated by the defendant. Dr. Matthews told me that the defendant was despondent. In the last phone call, he thanked Dr. Matthews for their long friendship, and asked him to pray for him after his death. I submitted this information in my report, on page six."

Kurkowski flipped through the pages of the report. "This is what Dr. Campbell told you? Dr. Campbell, a lifelong friend of the defendant, told you that the defendant thought he was dying. Isn't that what friends do? Don't friends try to cover for their friends?"

"Objection," said the defense counsel.

"State your objection," asked the judge.

"Your honor, the prosecutor is again asking compound questions and is leading the witness."

"Sustained. Ms Kurkowski, please state your question," said the judge.

"Yes, your honor. Dr. Forge, the defendant and Dr. Matthews were friends, lifelong friends, were they not?"

"Yes."

"Isn't it true that friends, especially lifelong friends, sometimes lie for their friends?"

"Yes."

"No further questions, your honor," Kurkowski said, as she left the lectern.

The judge asked, "Defense counsel, do you wish to re-direct?"

"Yes your honor."

The defense attorney, John Rada, was a young man who looked uncomfortable wearing a suit and tie. He awkwardly approached the lectern and shuffled a stack of papers for several minutes.

"We are waiting, counselor," said the judge.

"Yes, your honor. I apologize. "Uh, Dr. Forge, you testified that the defendant's dentist, Dr. Matthews, told you that he told the defendant that he was dying, is that correct?"

"Yes."

"Dr. Matthews also told you that the defendant called him twice, and asked Dr. Matthews to pray for him after his death?"

"Yes."

"So, both the defendant, and Dr. Matthews thought he was dying?"

"Objection. Hearsay, your honor," said Kurkowski.

Rada shuffled his papers. "Your honor, Dr. Matthews testified under oath, that he told the defendant that he was dying."

"Objection overruled. Continue, counselor," said the judge.

"Dr. Forge, do you have any other evidence that the defendant thought he was dying, and that his death was imminent?"

"Yes. When I spoke to his siblings, again, I interviewed them separately; they each told me that they had conversations with the defendant regarding his diagnosis. They both told me that the defendant thought he was going to die soon. They both said that they believed the defendant, and were making plans to try to visit him. Unfortunately, the siblings were having financial difficulties and could not afford to make the trip."

"Did the siblings tell you anything else, Dr. Forge?"

"Yes. They said the defendant told them that he expected to die before their grandmother died."

"Dr. Forge, didn't Dr. Matthews also testify that the defendant told him that he expected to die before his grandmother died?"

"Yes."

"Then what happened?"

"Lucas answered, "When his grandmother died first, he believed he would die within days, or perhaps a few hours, and expected that both of their bodies would be found in his house. When that did not happen after two days, he decided that his last act as a loving grandson would be to bury her, according to her expressed wish. Her decomposing body was setting off nauseating fumes. According to the coroner's report, when the police found the freezer, it appeared that she had been gently and carefully placed inside the freezer. He then took his grandmother's body to Sedona, by himself, because he did not want his siblings to get into trouble. His judgment at the time, of course, was compromised by his cocaine induced psychosis."

"No further questions, Your Honor."

Kurkowski's shoulders slumped ever so slightly.

"Your honor, the defense rests."

"In that case, Dr. Forge, thank you for your testimony. You are excused."

Stepping outside the courtroom, Lucas breathed a sigh of relief. He realized that he hated depositions and he hated testifying in court. Although he held great respect for the legal system, he decided then and there, that he needed to do something different with his life. More importantly, he remembered the promise that he made to his father, that he would serve his country. He needed to honor that promise.

Chapter 3

The Arroyos

Listening to a podcast on recent advances in neuroscience, Lucas Forge was well into his 30-minute cardio workout when the droning speaker's voice was interrupted by an incoming telephone call. Breathing heavily, he pushed the answer call button. In a silky baritone, he said, "Forge here."

"Dr. Forge, this is Detective Lindsay from the Maricopa County Sheriff's Office. Can I have a moment of your time?"

Lucas' mind sped through a myriad of possible reasons why the detective would be calling him on his private line. Choosing an interrogatory rather than an assent, he asked, "How did you get my number?"

Taken off guard, the detective hesitated for a beat and answered, "I spoke to the prosecutor on a case in which you were involved as an expert witness several years ago. Her name is…give me a minute. I have it right here. Kurkowski, Sheila Kurkowski. She recommended you and gave me your number."

Lifting an eyebrow, Lucas pictured Kurkowski's pinched face and remembered her gravelly voice. *Well, will wonders never cease?* "I see, Detective Lindsay. For what, exactly, did she recommend me?"

"Yes, right to the point. She said to expect that. I've been working on a case. Actually, it's a series of cases that seem to be related. We've reached a roadblock. I could use a pair of fresh eyes."

Lucas said, "Detective Lindsay, you said I, and then you said we. How many are involved in these series of cases?"

"Well, Dr. Forge, I'm the lead detective, but I was recently assigned to the case after several years of no progress, and the former lead detective is on permanent medical leave. I have two other case officers working with me."

Sensing the desperation in the man's voice, Lucas said, "Okay. Tell me more."

In a deep raspy tone, the detective continued. "We got a dead body problem. More accurately, we got a 'dead bodies' problem. Going back to 1970, the Maricopa County Medical Examiner's database lists more than 300 unidentified bodies. They're mostly male, mostly young, and mostly Latino. Some cases stem from the discovery of body parts, such as a skull or a femur. Some of them have IDs that turn out, of course, to be fake IDs."

Imagining a map of Maricopa County, Lucas said, "Maricopa County covers a lot of territory, detective. As I recall, it is almost ten thousand square miles of territory."

"You're right. It's nine thousand, two hundred and twenty four square miles, to be exact. I looked it up. But here's the kicker, nearly half of the bodies are found in and around the small town of Gila Bend. The town's population is only around two thousand souls."

Lucas pictured the small town in his mind. Gila Bend was an anachronism, a town in the middle of nowhere, a throwback to the 1960s. He remembered eating at the Space Age Lodge restaurant. The building was designed to look like a flying saucer. Like so many other small towns in the West, they once had delusions of grandeur mixed in with superstition, and Native American folklore.

The detective continued. "Gila Bend is about hundred miles north of the closest border point with Mexico. It's likely that many of the bodies are young men who crossed the border illegally and died in the harsh desert on their way to the 'Promised Land.' I can only surmise that drug and human trafficking are the main reasons for many of the bodies. But, a new pattern has emerged in the last several years."

Cocking his head, Lucas squinted in concentration. "I'm listening. Go on."

"Twelve of the most recent cases were young males, but only two were Latino. Each of the bodies was mutilated, torn apart with almost surgical precision. The remains were dumped in shallow graves, along several arroyos around Gila Bend. Coyotes, of the animal kind, destroyed most of the crime scenes. This new-fangled DNA testing has identified only one of the bodies. It was of a 17-year old runaway boy, originally from Chicago. We thought he was a male prostitute who met up with the wrong guy."

"So, you are assuming these twelve cases are related," Lucas said. "Is there enough evidence to suggest a serial killer is on the loose?"

"That's our working hypothesis." Detective Lindsay continued. "There's something more that connects the cases. The lab results have also found that in all twelve cases, there're some unusual chemicals found in each of the bodies."

"Unusual, in what way?" Lucas asked.

"We don't know. The lab guys think it's some kind of hallucinogenic and paralytic substance. The chemicals are in the same family of drugs used in shamanistic ceremonies, but they have never been used, or found, in North America. They think they come from South America, possibly as far south as Argentina."

"So, how may I be of assistance?"

"After Kurkowski recommended you, I checked you out. You've done some profiling work, you have some expertise in illicit drugs and drug running, and you identified that guy who murdered his grandmother and buried her in an arroyo."

Shaking his head, Lucas said, "You are correct on the first two items, but you are wrong about the third. That guy, to whom you are referring, did not murder his grandmother. She died of natural causes. Also, I did not identify him, at least not in the way you might be thinking."

"What do you mean?"

Lucas answered, "I was invited to the so-called crime scene, where the body was found. It was a shallow grave in an arroyo. The body washed up in a rain storm, but it had no identifying information on it."

"Then how did you find the killer?"

"As I said, the grandson did not kill her. While I was examining the body, the officers turned her over. Underneath the body, I spotted a business card stuck in the mud. It belonged to the grandson. He apparently took off his jacket to bury her, and the card fell out of his pocket. Profiling was not needed at that point."

"Wow. I wish we could get that lucky," said the detective.

"Sometimes luck trumps good detective work, and even science," Lucas said.

"And sometimes, we can take credit for our good fortune," added the detective.

Shaking his head, Lucas said, "You still have not answered my question. How may I be of assistance to you?"

"I'd like you to take a look at the evidence we have and maybe point us in a new direction. Maybe you could do your profiling thing and help us find this guy before he kills again. Maybe you could look at the crime scenes, and maybe your, uh, 'good luck', will find something we missed."

Closing his eyes, Lucas silently focused on the meager data provided by detective Lindsay.

After more than a minute passed, the detective asked, "Are you still there?"

Lucas answered, "Yes I am. I must say I am intrigued. When may I visit some of the body dumps?"

The detective smiled with relief. "I was hoping we could go out there in the morning, before it gets unbearably hot. I could pick you up if you tell me where you live."

After taking a moment, Lucas replied, "It will be more convenient for you, if I meet you at your office. We can leave from there, and when we return, I can look at your files. I wake up early every morning. May I meet you after sunrise, around six o'clock?"

"Yes, I'll meet you at six. I'm at the Surprise, Arizona office on West Bell Road and Dysart. And, Dr. Forge?" he continued, "Thank you."

"A thank you may be premature. We will see if I get lucky this time." Lucas disconnected the call. Resuming his cardio work out, he continued to examine the data in his mind. Finding no new patterns, he took a hot shower and got dressed. He spent the rest of the day in the library.

***

The next morning, he awakened early, at his usual time, long before the sun rose. Stepping outside in the pre-dawn air, he inhaled the acrid scent of mesquite and greasewood. A mockingbird was singing a tune that sounded a lot like a complex car alarm.

The constellation Orion was low in the southern sky. Lucas imagined connecting the star dots to envision Orion, the hunter of ancient lore with his hunting dogs, Canis Major and Canis Minor.

Lucas recalled the Greek myth of Orion who angered the earth goddess, Gaia by boasting he would kill all of the wild animals on earth. Gaia was the mother of all animals. Enraged, she sent an enormous scorpion after him. Neither his strength nor his sword could defeat the scorpion. When he tried to escape, the scorpion stung and killed Orion. As a reward for its service, Gaia then sent the scorpion to the sky, where the constellation Scorpio is seen still pursuing Orion.

Addressing Orion, Lucas thought, *The hunt is on.* Shifting his gaze toward Scorpio, he felt a chill creeping along his back.

***

Pulling into the parking lot of the Maricopa County Sheriff's office, Lucas checked his watch. It was 5:55. The building was a minimalist one story stucco structure with the ubiquitous red tile roof. The desert landscaping was still young, providing no shade from the brutal Arizona sun. Lucas found a north facing spot, hoping to shield his dashboard from the infra red solar radiation. Leaving the comfort of his air-conditioned vehicle, Lucas walked to the entrance of the building, through one of the three arches.

Quickly scanning the office for exits, as was his habit, he noticed several tan-uniformed MSCO deputies who were engaged in an animated conversation about their heroics in a recent arrest.

A skinny young man, with a badly pock-marked face, sat in an institutional metal chair next to an institutional metal desk. His hands were handcuffed behind him and his head hung down. The smell of burned coffee permeated the lobby.

Walking up to the front desk, Lucas tried to get the attention of the uniformed deputy who was busily filling out a form. "Good morning, officer. I am Dr.

Lucas Forge and I have an appointment with Detective Lindsay."

Without changing expression or acknowledging his presence, the deputy swiveled in his chair and punched a few numbers into the phone. In a few seconds, he spoke into the receiver, "Lindsay, a Dr. Forbes is here to see you." He hung up without waiting for a response and turned back to his paperwork. Lucas decided not to correct his mispronunciation of his name.

Hearing a buzz and a loud metallic click, Lucas turned to his left to see a medium sized, gray haired man walking through a doorway. The man had a decided limp and was wearing faded brown chino pants and a brown blazer. He sported a multi-colored yellowish-orange tie that had been loosened, or probably, never fully pulled up to his white collar. His black tactical boots made no sound on the tile floor. As the man ambled toward him, Lucas noticed the gold detective shield attached to the man's heavy black leather belt, and a bulge under his coat, likely a concealed pistol.

Looking around the lobby, he had a puzzled expression on his face. His eyes finally returned to Lucas, and they examined him up and down. Reaching out his right hand, the man smiled and asked hesitatingly, "Dr. Forge? I'm Detective Lindsay. Thank you for coming." His blue eyes matched his authentic smile.

Returning the smile, Lucas replied, "Nice to meet you in person, Detective Lindsay." He reached out his hand to shake it.

The detective's hand was warm and dry, and Lucas felt the calluses of a man unafraid of manual labor. His grip was strong, but not punishing.

The detective stared at Lucas face, before releasing his grip. "You are younger than I expected."

Lucas replied, "Yes, I hear that a lot."

Nodding, the detective asked, "Can I get you a cup of coffee before we go?"

"No thank you. I already drank a cup on the way here."

Glancing at the coffee station at the back of the lobby, the detective laughed and said, "Good choice. The sludge they make here is perfectly awful. Shall we go? Without waiting for a response, the detective slid past Lucas and limped out of the building, with Lucas trailing behind.

The detective opened the doors to a white SUV patrol car and started the engine. Cranking up the air conditioning, he told Lucas, "Buckle up." He pulled out onto Bell road and headed west to the 303 loop heading south. Watching the detective out of the corner of his eyes, Lucas waited patiently for the man to begin talking. The detective appeared to be lost in thought. It wasn't until they reached I-10 heading west that he began to speak.

"The last body was found a week ago. We should go to that location first."

"Do you have any idea how long the corpse was there?" Lucas asked.

"The ME estimated that it had been decomposing for at least two months. We haven't had much rain, but the coyotes tore things up pretty bad. We found less than half of the body. It appears to have been a 16 or 17 year old Latino boy. There was no ID or anything we could use to trace his identity."

"I noticed there are wooden crosses in the back seat. What are those for?" Lucas asked.

The detective frowned, and replied, "Gila Bend has a contract with us to provide policing services. The previous lead detective on this case had this idea to put up these crosses whenever and wherever we find a body. They have numbers on them and our phone number. We are starting to use GPS coordinates to keep track of their locations. There is a map in the glove box pinpointing all of the crosses." His face darkened.

Turning toward the detective, Lucas asked, "I sense there is more to it than you are telling me."

"Yeah, you're right. My predecessor, Detective Lewis, was hoping the crosses would serve as a deterrent to any illegals or drug runners crossing the desert. Frankly, I'm not sure it's having any effect. It's beginning to look like a cemetery out there. The number of illegals keeps increasing, and I haven't seen much of a decline in drugs crossing the border. The desert is being destroyed by all the trash these people leave behind. They sure don't have any respect for the environment."

"Anymore than they have respect for our laws," Lucas noted.

Detective Lindsay took a long look at Lucas.

"What?" Lucas asked.

"I don't know. I guess I figured all you shrinks are liberals."

Lucas laughed. "Well, to be honest. I started out as pretty liberal. I even had some socialist thinking when I was young, well, 'younger', and in college."

"What changed you?"

"My father insisted I serve our country. I was exposed to real life outside the classroom. I saw how socialism failed wherever it was tried and how it really wasn't much different from fascism. I saw how much peopled suffered under socialism and how few opportunities to succeed they had. Then a big turning point was when a wise man told me to look at the words on a penny."

"Words? What words?"

"There are three words or phrases on a US penny. In God We Trust, E Pluribus Unum, and Liberty. These are the foundations of the unique system of government we call the United States. I learned that our freedom and rights come from God, not government. Many of our founding fathers believed that if we did not have God in our lives, that we could not sustain the republic. E Pluribus Unum, or 'out of many, one', means that there is an American way of life, and an American value system. People of many different backgrounds can assimilate. Liberty is the idea that no matter our background, we can choose to go as far in life as our abilities can take us."

"I guess I missed that day in school," the detective said.

"I'm not sure that is even taught in any school anymore," Lucas replied.

Both men were silent for a long while. Looking to the right, outside of his window, Lucas saw the tall light poles and barbed wire fencing that surrounded the Lewis State Prison complex. He wondered at all the laws that must have been broken by the broken men inside.

A few minutes later, the detective announced, "We are coming into Gila Bend. A few of the bodies were found to the right, where you can see the arroyos coming down from the mountains. Most of them were found to the south of the town, in the open desert arroyos."

Passing through the town at the posted 35 mph speed limit, Lucas marveled that none of the other vehicles passed their marked Sheriff's SUV. There was a long line of cars behind them. The town had not changed much. A few more businesses were closed down, and a newer Texaco gas and food mart seemed to be the place to hang out for the younger crowd.

The detective drove to the end of the town and then under the I-8 overpass, following the two-lane highway with open desert on both sides. After driving a few miles, he turned right onto a dirt road heading deep into the mesquite and Palo Verde trees. The bouncy road was not maintained and consisted of potholes, rocks and washboard surfaces. After a few miles, the detective pulled off to the right. They were now overlooking a shallow arroyo that ran from the north to the south.

"Watch out for the cholla," the detective warned.

Lucas stepped carefully around the dangerous yellow cactus that looked almost huggable from a distance.

They slid their way down the sides of the arroyo to the rocky river bottom. There were no traces of moisture anywhere. Heading north a few hundred feet, they came upon one of the white crosses. A mound of sand and rocks marked what once was the temporary grave for a boy without a future. A red-tailed hawk circled in a thermal above their heads.

"We couldn't find any useful footprints. There were signs of digging and some pieces of plastic from a construction-grade garbage bag that you can buy at hundreds of stores around the valley. This was the case I investigated, when I took over from Detective Lewis."

"You said he was on medical leave. What happened to him?" Lucas asked.

Detective Lindsay turned to the south and pointed. "A few miles south of here, Lewis was patrolling and saw a vehicle down one of the dirt roads. He called it in before he could get a license plate or vehicle make. That was his last transmission. When he didn't respond, two deputies came out here to find him." The detective looked down at the ground and kicked at the sand. His hands balled into fists.

"What happened?"

"They found him with his head bashed in. It looked like he was attacked from behind. He was still alive and they air evac'd him to the level one trauma center in Phoenix. We think he was hit with a shovel. He's never come out of his coma. We may never know what happened."

They visited three more white crosses before returning to the office. Lucas could find no helpful clues or patterns at any of the sites.

Lucas spent the rest of the afternoon looking through the meager files on all of the unidentified victims. The thickest file was the most recent one. They obtained a photograph of the boy from his family in Chicago. He looked younger than his years. Lucas noted that there was something different about the boy's hairstyle and his smile. He looked almost effeminate.

Pushing himself away from the desk, he closed his eyes and remained that way for nearly ten minutes. Detective Lindsay waited patiently for him to speak.

Finally, Lucas opened his eyes and looked at the detective. Shaking his head slowly, he said, "I am afraid I cannot be of much help. I can only give you hypotheses, based on national statistics, and the meager data we have here."

"I'll take whatever you got."

Lucas began, "You appear to have a killer, most likely a white male, in his late twenties or thirties, but possibly older. He is likely well-educated. He has familiarity with human anatomy. He may have had some experience in the medical field. He has some connection with South America. He likely has some connection with the drug trade, possibly even the cartels. He likes to dominate and incapacitate his victims. He is attracted to young males, especially those with darker skin. He is conflicted about his own sexuality, possibly enraged at his own sexual urges and preferences. He may have been punished as a child for homosexual acts. He likely has achieved success in life to compensate for his inadequacies, and/or to prove himself to a critical, domineering, authoritarian parent."

The detective was nodding, and writing as fast as he could.

"Don't worry. I'll type it up for you," Lucas said.

"Thank you. Is there anything else?"

Nodding sadly, Lucas replied, "Yes. He's not done yet. I recommend staking out the arroyos. He doesn't want to be caught. You may not be able to take him alive."

They two men stood and shook hands. Lucas turned away silently and walked slowly to his vehicle. He knew his dreams would be haunted for many nights.

Chapter 4   Two months Earlier

The craving in his gut was sending rivulets of pain up through his chest, around his shoulders, down his arms, and ending at his fingertips. Looking at the broad back of the impeccably dressed older man standing at the wet bar, Jeffrey Elisandro wanted this to be over quickly, but the man seemed to be in no hurry. Sitting on the edge of the bed in the posh hotel suite, Jeffrey tried to distract himself by surveying the bedroom decorations.

His right leg, bouncing up and down like a sewing machine needle, sent a vibration through the firm mattress. Part of his mind marveled at the attention to detail the room's decorators had devoted to making the room look like something one might find in an expansive mansion.

Looking over his shoulder toward Jeffrey, Alexander Broadbent was feeling his own craving rise up through his loins. Jeffrey, if that was his real name, looked almost angelic, with his thick blond hair framing his smooth dark skin and his long thin nose that was bracketed by those intensely blue eyes. The young boy's lanky frame, long legs, and apparent nervousness excited him. The black-haired man momentarily drifted, imagining himself cradling that precious face in his hands and losing himself in those blue eyes.

Regaining control, Alexander's deep baritone voice asked, "Do you prefer scotch or vodka?"

Jumping at the sound, Jeffrey forced himself back into his character, as the shy, fragile, innocent waif he was supposed to portray. Over the past several months, he had developed and practiced several characters that would appeal to the varied tastes of the older men he seduced for money.

Sometimes, he took on the role of a nubile gang member. Other times, he was the bookish high school nerd, wearing a gaming t-shirt and plaid shorts. His current role seemed to attract the wealthier johns, like the man standing at the wet bar.

Looking up coyly though his blond bangs, and slowly brushing the hair out of his eyes with his left hand, he asked, "Uh, do you have any wine?"

Smiling, Alexander stared into the boys eyes, holding the gaze longer than would be polite in other circumstances. "Red or white? I have a nice Malbec you might enjoy."

Retuning the gaze and then shyly looking down, Jeffrey answered with a hint of uncertainty, "Uh, okay. I'll have a glass of, uh, that."

Turning back toward the bar, Alexander smiled. *I am going to enjoy this one.* Selecting a bottle from the wine rack, he smoothly inserted the bottle into the granite-based Frontgate wine opener. Pulling the handle, he removed the cork slowly, in what he hoped would appear to be seductive to young Jeffrey.

Reaching for the decanter, he stopped himself, selecting a wine glass instead. *He will not know the difference anyway.*

Pouring a generous glass for the boy, he let it sit while he opened the 21 year old Balvenie single malt, and poured three fingers for himself into the crystal glass. Lifting the glass to his nose, he inhaled the smoky aroma. Lowering the glass to his lips, he turned toward the boy, looking into his eyes as he took a large sip. The smooth scotch rewarded his refined palate.

Picking up the wine glass in his other hand, he moved gracefully toward the bed. Stopping in front of Jeffrey, he stood close, inside the boy's personal space. Offering the glass to him, he watched hungrily as Jeffrey took the glass using both of his trembling hands. Pushing the glasses together, a soft clink rang out.

Walking back nonchalantly toward the bar, and reaching into his pocket, Alexander found the small box and the nitrile glove. With his back to the boy, he set his glass on the counter. Quickly slipping the glove onto his right hand and flipping the lid open with his fingers, he rubbed his index finger into the sticky substance.
Carefully closing the box, he slipped it back into his pocket, Picking up his scotch with his left hand, and keeping his right hand hidden behind him, he moved slowly, back toward the boy.

Oh crap; here he comes, Jeffrey noticed, with a touch of disgust. Putting on his best shy smile, and shaking his hair out of his eyes, he looked up at the smiling man. *He looks like a wolf. I hope he doesn't bite me.* Taking a large gulp of the wine, he downed half of the glass.

Alexander sat on the bed next to the boy, making sure their thighs touched. Gently, he reached his right arm around Jeffrey's shoulders, pulling him closely. Looking down at the top of the boy's head and enjoying the shine on the boy's hair. He slowly moved his right hand next to the boy's neck. Curling his index finger, he rubbed the substance into the boy's skin as if he were beginning to caress him.

Jeffrey, trying to play his role, reached up to place his hand softly over the man's fingers. Touching the hand, and feeling the plastic glove, his internal alarm went off. Stiffening, he thought, *What the fuck is that? What does he have on his hand?*

Starting to stand up and back away, Jeffrey was horrified to find he could not move his legs. His arms were frozen in place. *Holy shit, the old bastard drugged me! But how? I watched him pour the wine into the glass.* He noticed that he could still move his eyes, and that his lungs were still working. He could feel his heart thumping away rapidly inside his chest. Trying to speak, to scream, was useless. Nothing else in his body worked.

Standing up slowly, Alexander pried the glass of wine from the boy's stiffened grip. *Yes, it really works as advertised. I am going to find so many uses for this special drug.*

Drifting into memories of his own youth, Alexander Broadbent realized that he was a man used to manipulating others. As a child, he took great pleasure in capturing, imprisoning and torturing insects. He would bully and, if necessary, beat younger classmates into submission.

Alarmed by his frightening behavior, his mother took him to a family counselor, a young and eager licensed social worker, who tried to bond with little Alexander. She thought she was successful, but the boy merely honed his skills in human manipulation during their sessions. He told her what she wanted to hear and praised her faulty insights into his behavior. When she was not looking, he stole various small objects from her office, something she did not discover until months later.

Upon her recommendation, his parents purchased a guinea pig and a small terrarium with a little running wheel and a yellow ceramic house where it could sleep. They hoped Alexander would learn to bond with the furry creature and learn to care for it. He named it Piglet, from a Winnie the Pooh storybook. A few days later, Piglet mysteriously disappeared.

Alexander forced out fake tears by poking himself in his eyes. His mother tried to console him, while his father stood looking at the boy's face. His father, a policeman, was not so easily fooled. Staring at the boy's face as he sobbed in his mother's arms, his father recognized the coldness behind the boy's eyes. He had seen it many times in the clever criminals he had encountered in his undercover operations.

They took Alexander to a psychiatrist, who hurried through a thirty minute examination of the boy. At the end of the short interview, he took out a prescription pad and wrote out a prescription for a new drug, one not yet approved for children. Alexander pretended to take the pills, and acted more sweetly around his parents, and also with the psychiatrist, during the monthly fifteen minutes prescription renewal sessions.

The smug psychiatrist felt like a hero, whose brilliant medicinal intervention saved another lost boy. Many months later, he noticed that he too was missing items from his office, including a prescription pad. The psychiatrist, a middle aged man with a very busy practice, was reprimanded by his licensing board, and humiliated by the DEA investigation into his loss of the prescription pad.

Alexander learned to forge prescriptions and was able to obtain different medications when his mother took him to the nearby pharmacy. She was so relieved at the apparent changes in her son, that she never questioned the changes in medications, assuming the psychiatrist knew what he was doing.

Alexander changed his tactics at school. Instead of being the bully, he was now a young entrepreneur, selling prescription mood altering drugs to his eager customers. He felt a growing sense of superiority over his peers, especially when they were older students.

High school opened up new possibilities and new markets. Alexander expanded his supply of pharmaceuticals to include non-prescription drugs that he obtained from local dealers. He learned to give away samples, always smiling conspiratorially and whispering, "The first one is free." Soon he would charge them exorbitant prices for the same drugs, making a huge profit for himself. He never used the drugs himself, seeing how his customers would descend into apathy and lose control of their minds and ambition.

Alexander's father was often gone for weeks at a time, doing his undercover work. His mother busied herself with charity work, and would be absent from home when Alexander returned from school. They never questioned or monitored his growing bank balances. Alexander was not interested in the video games his peers seemed to enjoy. He preferred the real violence he could inflict upon the animals he found wandering the streets.

Despising his teachers, he rarely completed their silly homework assignments; either paying others to complete his work, or studying hard the night before a test. His brilliant mind could easily absorb and remember information, so he nearly always aced his exams. He preferred to study on his own, searching for books and courses on business, marketing and entrepreneurship.

Despite his success in school, he never made any real friends. Girls seemed to be afraid of him. He liked one boy and tried to be friends, but the boy rejected him, calling him a faggot. He fantasized about killing that boy.

Leaving home as soon as he turned eighteen, he rented his first house, a large four bedroom home near a college campus. Taking the master suite for himself, he rented the other three rooms to college students, charging them enough so that he could pay the monthly bills without having to spend any of his own money. His parents were secretly relieved to have him gone, and the feeling was mutual.

Being near a college campus was extremely lucrative. Even some professors became his customers. Then he had his first run in with the law. Having sold some OxyContin pills to an undercover narcotics officer, his house was raided by a multiagency task force in the middle of the night. He happened to be up late, doing some research, when his front door was smashed in, and a dozen armed officers, dressed in riot gear burst into his living room. Shouting and waving their guns around, he and his roommates were forced to the ground and handcuffed, while his house was torn apart.

Alexander was too smart to store any drugs or paraphernalia in his own residence, so they found nothing incriminating. His father, still an undercover officer himself, was furious with him when he found out his own son was on the wrong side of the law. They ended their relationship after brutal argument.

Alexander already had a high-priced attorney on his payroll, so he only spent a few silent hours in the interview room at the jail. Refusing to answer any questions until his attorney was present, he was soon released. His attorney was later able to get the case dismissed on several technicalities. Instead of monetary reimbursement, he gladly accepted a kilo of cocaine for his services.

Adapting as he always did to changing circumstances, Alexander became even more careful. He hired layers of underlings to work his customers, some collecting the money upfront, while others distributed the product at a different time and location. He created separate cells among them, so that no one ever knew the others. Consequently if they were caught, the authorities could never trace anything back to him. He enjoyed the game of devising ways to avoid ever being caught again.

Soon, he began diversifying into legitimate businesses, sometimes only as a means to launder his massive amounts of cash, other times as new sources of revenue. It was never enough for him. He still had his hidden unquenchable urges that could be not be satisfied with power, drugs or money.

There was much more, but for now, his attention turned back to the young man in front of him.

Finishing his scotch, while becoming increasing aroused at Jeffrey's helplessness, he felt a rush of pleasure from the anticipation in his chest. Walking backwards with the two glasses, he gazed excitedly at the boy's lithe form. Jeffrey was still sitting in the same position as if he were a mime, one hand floating as if he was holding a glass, and the other hand almost touching his shoulder.

Placing the glasses on the counter behind him, Alexander returned to the room. Reaching into the walk-in closet, he rolled his carry-on bag over to the side of the bed. Lifting it onto the bed behind the boy, and slowing unzipping it, he lifted the lid. Staring briefly at the contents, he removed a leather briefcase and a blue plastic sheet. After zipping up the bag, he set it back on the floor and pushed it away from the bed a few feet.

Lifting his briefcase and the plastic sheet, he walked into the tiled master bathroom, knelt down and spread the sheet onto the cold tile floor. He opened the briefcase, smiling at the gleaming metal instruments inside. Returning to the bedroom, he began removing his clothes, folding them neatly, and placing them on the edge of the bed.

Jeffrey was screaming silently. A tear, born out of abject terror, escaped his left eye and drifted slowly down his smooth cheek.

Chapter 4 Two Months Earlier

Chapter 5

The Next Morning

Entering the elevator with his two large wheeled suitcases, Alexander Broadbent felt relieved that no one was around this early in the morning. It was still dark outside, and the Arizona sun would not make its appearance for several more hours. Pushing the button for P2, Alexander waited for the doors to close before he could exhale.

Lurching to a halt, the elevator's doors opened. Harsh florescent lights flickered dimly overhead, revealing the gray walls and pillars of the parking garage. Stepping through the doors, he pulled the two heavy suitcases over the ridge at the base of the elevator.

The odor of wet mesquite and cement lingered in the air. Quickly looking around to make sure he was alone, he pulled the hood of his sweatshirt over his head and rolled the suitcases to the back of his black 4WD Chevy Suburban. Opening the rear doors, he lifted the suitcases into the rear compartment and quietly closed the doors.

Looking around at the ceiling, he checked once more to ensure there were no cameras. Satisfied, he crawled into the driver's seat and started the engine. Backing up slowly, he turned the wheels and exited the garage.

Traffic was very light at this time of the morning, even on the heavily travelled Pima Road. He drove south at five miles an hour above the speed limit, so as to not draw any suspicion to himself. Looking at the small black box on the dashboard, he confirmed that his radar detector was working. Even though he had filled the tank the night before, he checked the gauge anyway. *Leave nothing to chance*, he reminded himself.

Turning west onto I-10, Alexander was surprised to find the traffic was heavier. Convoys of 18 wheelers rolled their way east and west to unknown destinations. Alexander merged into a center lane and repeatedly checked his speed and the gauges on his dash. Pushing a few buttons, he was pleased to hear classical music filling the cabin. *Ah...Isle of the Dead, by Rachmaninov. How apropos.*

Almost 40 miles later, he exited onto highway 85, heading south to Gila Bend. It was still dark, but the sky in the east was beginning to pale. The highway was dampened from a recent rain, and Alexander smiled to himself. *That will make digging much easier.*

Twenty minutes later, he was driving slowly through the historic town of Gila Bend. He smiled, shaking his head in amusement as he drove past the Space Age Lodge and restaurant, with its UFO style roof. He could not imagine ever staying there. Gila Bend was a dump of a town, filled with backwards yokels, Indians, and a growing population of Mexicans, probably mostly illegal immigrants who had risked crossing the deadly deserts of Arizona to find work in El Norte.

Continuing past the end of town, Alexander headed south into the empty landscape. A few miles later, he found a small dirt road heading west. No one was on the highway, so he turned right and headed into the desert. Switching the Suburban into 4 wheel drive, he drove slowly.

After bumping along for a few more miles, he pulled off to the right, where the dirt road widened near a wash. Turning off the engine, he stepped out of his Suburban and listened, while he surveyed his surroundings. He could hear the faint roar of the 18 wheelers, barreling down I-8, heading east toward Casa Grande. The sand and gravel beneath his feet was wet, but not squishy.

Grabbing his blue nitrile gloves and a shovel, and locking his vehicle, he headed into the desert wash to find a suitable spot begging for a body dump. He passed by a small cross with a number on it.

Thinking back, he remembered reading that a disproportionate number of dead bodies had been found in the desert around Gila Bend. The crosses were placed where bodies were found by the Maricopa County Sheriff's Office. The crosses were supposed to serve two purposes. One was to deter would-be desert crossers. *Abandon all hope, ye who enter here*, he chuckled to himself. The other purpose served to more easily send help, by providing a location, as each numbered cross was linked to a specific GPS coordinate.

The wash had mounds of soft sand that had shifted with the wind and the occasional flash floods. *Perfect*, he mused. Leaving the shovel and returning to the vehicle, Alexander unlocked the rear doors and removed one of the suitcases. Carrying, rather than dragging it, he returned to the wash and unzipped the bag. Stuffed into the plastic inside were some of the remains of the boy who entertained him last night.

Lifting the bag out of the suitcase, he dropped the plastic bag next to one of the sandy mounds. Returning to the vehicle, he left the empty suitcase and he repeated the process with the second suitcase. In a short time, he had dug a shallow grave. After emptying the contents of the bags into the hole, he rolled up the bloody plastic into a tight bundle.

Covering the grave took less time than digging it. The sun was almost up. The clouds to the east were painted in pinks and grays, interspersed with patches of blue sky. Alexander always loved those colors. For a brief moment, he felt alive again. The scent of the wet mesquite was intoxicating. Removing the nitrile gloves, he replaced them with a clean set. Shoving the plastic bundle and his soiled gloves into a fresh black garbage bag, he tied it shut and returned to his vehicle, placing the suitcase, gloves, shovel, and garbage bag into the back of the Suburban.

He stopped suddenly when he heard the sounds of an approaching vehicle. Grabbing the shovel, he ran and hid behind a Palo Verde tree. He watched a tall man in a sheriff's uniform approach his Suburban.

***

Returning to Gila Bend, he pulled into the Texaco at the southern edge of town. Driving around back, he stopped next to a large dumpster. Finding no one around, he quickly got out of his vehicle, removed the garbage bag and gloves, and tossed them into the dumpster. Jumping back into the Suburban, he headed back to Scottsdale. The excitement and elation of the previous evening was replaced by smug satisfaction. *I got away with another one.*

Back on highway 85, as he drove past the Lewis prison, he surveyed the empty desert surrounding the complex. He began to feel the gnawing pangs of emptiness growing inside. He wasn't hungry for breakfast.

Chapter 6

The Agency

Lucas arrived early for his appointment with the Director. He knew the Director was a fastidious perfectionist. The nature of the meeting was not revealed to him, so he prepared as if he were meeting the Pope. His suit was cleaned and pressed, he wore a new white button-down shirt, a conservative tie and his shoes were highly polished. His face was tanned from spending the weekend outdoors without his shirt.

The Director's secretary, Cecelia, offered him coffee, but he declined, not knowing if the Director would approve. He asked her if she knew the purpose of the meeting, but she replied in her soft British accent, "I am sorry, Dr. Forge. I am not privy to that information." Lucas suspected that she was not being entirely truthful, but he appreciated her discretion.

There was nothing to read, so Lucas concentrated on remembering a few lines from Epictetus' <u>Meditations</u>. A few minutes later, Cecelia's intercom beeped.

"Send him in, please," said the voice.

"Yes sir," Cecelia replied, reaching over to push a hidden button under her desk. "You may go in now, Dr. Forge" she said to Lucas.

The lock on the door buzzed, he turned the handle, entering the well furnished office. Standing next to the Director's desk was the mountain of a man Lucas instantly recognized as Agent Jake Holstein. The Director remained seated in a large leather chair behind his heavy mahogany desk. The Director did not look up, but remained focused on the thick file folder in front of him.

Lucas approached the desk and waited. He stole a glance at Agent Holstein, who only smiled thinly back at him. After a full minute, the Director lowered the file and stared unsmilingly at Lucas over the top of his reading glasses. Lucas felt a bead of sweat roll down his spine. He kept his face in neutral, as the sweat trickled lower.

The Director began, "Dr. Lucas Forge."

"Yes sir," Lucas said.

"You are awfully young to be in this position," he stated flatly. Lucas did not respond, as he did not hear a question.

"Agent Holstein here thinks you may be of some use to us," the Director said.

"I am at your service, Director, sir."

"Yes, of course you are. How is your Spanish?"

"Well, sir. As you know, I spent a long time serving in Panama. I picked up the dialect pretty quickly. I am told I have an ear for languages."

"I hope so, as we need you to learn other dialects. Specifically, we need you to learn Argentine dialects. Is that a problem?"

"I enjoy learning new dialects sir."

The Director visually examined him from head to toe, as if he were buying a race horse. "Where do you see yourself in five years, Dr. Forge?"

"I suspect I may be in Argentina, or wherever else I may be of service, sir."

Holstein stifled a laugh, drawing a harsh look from the Director.

Turning back to Lucas, the Director continued, "I see you were trained as a psychologist, but then served in Spec Ops. You were involved in several firefights and performed with distinction. You have also interrogated some high level drug lords and obtained valuable information from them. Don't you see a disconnect between being a psychologist and being a warrior?"

Lucas thought quickly. He had examined his own mind and values many times over the last three years. This was the same question he had asked himself. He was satisfied that he had arrived at a good answer.

He responded, "Sir, I believe successful warriors are also good psychologists. We have to know and understand our enemy. We have to know and understand their motivations and their weaknesses. Some battles and wars are fought and won without firing a bullet."

Unexpectedly, the Director laughed heartily. "Damn, Forge. That was an excellent answer. Good man." Turning to Holstein, he continued, "I believe you are correct in your assessment."

The Director stood up, and reached out his hand to Lucas. He was shorter than Lucas thought he was, and Lucas had to lean in to shake his hand. The Director's grip was powerful. "Welcome aboard, Dr. Forge. Here's to a long and beneficial relationship."

"Thank you, sir."

Turning to Agent Holstein, the Director said, "Take it from here, Agent. I will expect regular progress reports from you."

Holstein responded, "Yes, sir, of course, sir."

Holstein stood there, shifting his weight back and forth.

Finally the Director said, "Jesus, Holstein. We are done here. Get moving."

Straightening up, Agent Holstein saluted, "Yes sir, we are gone sir."

The salute was not returned. Lucas followed Holstein quickly out of the office. Cecelia was typing furiously, her eyes glued to some document. Lucas noticed a faint smile on her face.

"Have a smashing day, Cecelia. Cherrio," Lucas said.

Without lifting her eyes, she responded, "Good day, Dr. Forge; Agent Holstein."

The two men hurried out of her office. Cecelia looked up, watching them go. She smiled to herself. Once in the elevator, Holstein spoke, "I think that went well."

Lucas did not reply, but merely looked at the large man's face. He detected a sense of relief.

Holstein said, "Hey, Lucas, any day you meet with the Director and escape without a severe drumming down, it's a good day."

"What happens now, Jake?"

Smiling, Jake replied, "Pack your kit, Lucas. We're going to Argentina on a 0600 flight tomorrow."

Lucas noted that Jake's smile did not reach his eyes.

***

Unfastening his seatbelt, Lucas stood and stretched. The seats in the military aircraft were stingily padded. The aircraft had refueled at the Homestead Air Force base in Miami, but they were not allowed to leave the plane. They were now somewhere over the Caribbean and it was almost noon, Washington, DC time.

Lucas heard loud snoring emanating from Holstein's throat. Holstein's bulk was pretzeled across three seats, and a thin stream of drool wormed its way down his square jaw. A half dozen men sat at the front of the aircraft, as far as they could get from Holstein. They were engaged in a lively discussion, but Lucas could not hear their words.

Working his way to the back of the plane, Lucas opened the heavy door to the rear cargo hold. He was met by a blast of cold air. Several vehicles were strapped down, facing backwards, toward the loading ramp. Large wooden crates were stacked up on both sides of the hold.

Despite the cold, Lucas removed his fatigue jacket and shirt and folded them on top of the nearest crate. He was relieved to be alone. Bending over from his waist, he touched the toes of his tactical boots, stretching the stiff muscles in his lower back. For the next twenty minutes, he ran through an abbreviated set of exercises, until a thin film of sweat covered his face and muscular arms.

The aircraft suddenly lurched and banked steeply. Lucas went almost weightless and fell against one of the crates, grabbing a strap to steady himself. Hanging on, he waited until the wings were leveled. Quickly looking around the cavernous cargo hold, Lucas spotted several dozen parachute packs hanging on the walls. They were swinging back and forth as the plane continued to bounce.

"What are you doing back here?" shouted Holstein.

Lucas turned and saw Jake standing in the doorway, hanging on to the gray metal door frame. His bulk filled doorway, and the man had to bend over to get his head and shoulders through the entrance. "Christ. It's cold and noisy back here," he said. "Why is your shirt off?"

"I needed to get some exercise," Lucas answered.

Jake gave him a hard look. "You're going to get plenty of exercise in a few hours," he said, looking at his watch. "Save your strength. Get back in here. Briefing in ten minutes."

***

Night had fallen by the time the aircraft touched down at the General José de San Martin airport in Posadas, Argentina. The aircraft taxied to a remote area of the airport. Looking out the small windows, Lucas could see the lights of the city filtering through tall trees surrounding the airstrip. On the ground, several military vehicles were speeding toward the rear of the aircraft.

Holstein was already standing and heaving a heavy pack over his broad shoulders. He slipped a sling carrying his rifle over his neck, so that it hung down at the ready in front of his barrel chest. The other six men were in the aisles in various stages of following his lead. Lucas grabbed his rifle and kit and slipped into the straps as Holstein opened the door to the cargo hold.

Following on Holstein's heels, Lucas heard the mechanical whine of the loading ramp creeping downward. As they moved closer to the opening, Lucas felt the hot humid air strike his face. The odors of jet fuel exhaust were intermingled with fragrant jungle mist.

"Christ, it's hotter than New Orleans in July," Holstein complained pushing himself through the thick air.

A Jeep with four men in military fatigues pulled up to the base of the ramp. It was followed by two troop carriers with green canvas roofs. Lucas noted that none of the men in the Jeep wore any insignias or metal signifying rank, but one tall man was obviously in charge. He jumped out of the Jeep, stormed up to Holstein, and started shouting angrily in Spanish, inches from Jake's face. Holstein started shouting back, accusing the man of unspeakable acts with animals.

Without raising the barrel of his rifle, Lucas snapped the safety off and took an offensive posture. Holstein and the man stopped their shouting and both turned their heads toward Lucas. Lucas quickly looked toward the other three men who were just standing next to the jeep, with their hands on their own rifles. Their rifles were pointing downward.

Holstein and the man started laughing and grabbed each other in a hug. Holstein lifted the man off of his feet and turned, facing Lucas before putting the man down.

"Safety that weapon, Lucas," Holstein commanded. "This is my good friend, Captain Vega."

Feeling his face reddening, Lucas secured his rifle, ignoring the laughter of Vega's men.

Shaking his head, Vega said, "Jake, you bastard. You're going to get me killed one of these days. You must be more careful in briefing your men."

"Oh hell, what's the fun in that? I like keeping them on their toes. Vega, let me introduce Lucas, one of the new guys. Lucas, this is Captain Vega, and his men from the 12th Jungle Brigade."

Vega pushed himself away from Jake and reached out a hand toward Lucas. Lucas, throwing an evil look at Jake, shook Vega's hand, and muttered a greeting. Vega dropped his smile, but did not drop his grip, and looked hard into Lucas' eyes. Lucas stared back, taking in the measure of the man. The contest was broken by Jake.

"Hey guys, break it up. We have work to do."
Turning back to the rest of the team, Holstein waved his arm and said, "Unload the vehicles and crates."

Vega shouted to his men, "Dismount and give them a hand." A dozen men in fatigues piled out of the troop carriers.

The men introduced themselves to each other, while Jake and Vega stepped aside and spoke to each other in hushed tones.

Once the vehicles were unloaded and the crates secured, Jake said, "Okay men, mount up and follow the Captain."

They drove for an hour into the dense jungle on a bumpy dirt road. Lucas had to keep ducking under branches from trees that were struggling to reclaim the road. His shirt was drenched from sweat. Vega's Jeep finally pulled off to the left into a large flat clearing. Several trucks and Jeeps were parked in the back.

Two long tents with open sides sheltered tables with benches, a third tent held a field kitchen. Gas lanterns were strategically placed on the tables, attracting large flying insects. A couple of men were bustling around inside the kitchen. Sniffing the air, Lucas smelled the delicious aroma of grilled beef. His stomach did a flip-flop, and he suddenly realized he was very hungry.

Vega moved into the kitchen and spoke briefly to the two men. Turning back, he spoke to the Americans, "Please have a seat at the tables. We have to nourish ourselves before heading into the jungle. My men will take care of the equipment."

Jake and Vega sat across from each other at the end of one of the tables. Lucas took a seat that gave him a view of Vega's face. The other men quickly sat down as well. Several of the Argentine soldiers started passing out large bowls of bread and a simple salad with lettuce, tomatoes and onions. Smaller bowls contained hearts of palm and sliced avocados. Several bottles of a green sauce were placed on the tables.

"What's in the bottles?" asked Frank, another new-guy American. He was a short, thick, Italian-looking fellow, with huge calloused hands, and bright blue eyes. On the flight over, Jake said the guy was a mechanical genius and could fix anything from diesel engines to M-16s to claymore anti-personnel mines.

Lucas poured a little of the sauce on a fingertip and tasted it. "I think it is chimichurri sauce. You'll like it. It has garlic in it." Frank's face lit up with a huge smile. Lucas continued, "I think it also has red pepper, Italian parsley, cumin, and cilantro."

Frank continued smiling, and said, "You had me at garlic."

A soldier started to put bottles of wine on the table. Jake looked at Vega and frowned. Vega waved him off smiling and said to everyone, "One glass each. You must have a glass of Argentine Malbec with our Argentine steak."

Jake stood up and added loudly, "He said one glass each, men. That's all. One glass."

Frank groaned as his smile disappeared. He whispered, "Every party has a pooper."

The wine was poured and everyone had a sip just as the steaks arrived. After a few brief sounds of excitement, no one spoke for the next fifteen minutes as they devoured the meal. The plates were cleared as one of the cooks brought out individual servings of flan de leche.

Frank stuck a spoonful into his mouth and said loudly, "I officially defect to the 12th Jungle Brigade."

Captain Vegas smiled thinly and said, "Let us see if you still think so tomorrow."

The Argentine soldiers had set up three barracks tents with cots, while the American's were eating. Now it was their turn to eat. Holstein stood up and said, "Okay men. Time to get some shut eye. We will reassemble at 0300."

Checking his watch, Frank said, "That's only four hours from now."

Lucas replied, "Well, we better hit the sack."

The Americans pushed themselves away from the table. Frank looked around, and when no one was watching, he grabbed an unopened bottle of Malbec, and stuffed it inside of his shirt. Walking to the tent, he sniffed his armpit and said, "Damn. I stink."

Lucas grinned, "So what's new?"

Frank chased him into the tent. They were both asleep in ten minutes. Fortunately, Lucas fell asleep first, as Frank snored even louder than Holstein.

Chapter 7   The Jungle

It was the blackest night Lucas had ever seen. The sky was overcast with thick clouds that even the full moon could not penetrate. It was ninety degrees and the humidity was well over eighty percent. They had been climbing through the jungle, with only one short break for two hours. He trudged forward, relying on his hearing to follow Jake Holstein's soft footfalls in the darkness.

Suddenly, he felt a heavy hand on his shoulder, squeezing twice. It was Holstein, signaling him to stop and crouch down. He reached back, finding Frank's shoulder and repeated the message. Breathing through his nose, he exhaled quietly through his mouth. He felt sweat trickling down into his boots. Straining his eyes, he tried to peer into the darkness, but could only see faint outlines of dark gray on black.

He heard faint movement in front of him, and then whispers. After a few moments, he sensed Jake's head next to his. In a barely audible tone, Jake whispered, "We found them. Ten tangos at 10 o'clock. Vega's team is moving forward to flank them. Point in and wait until they open fire."

Lucas didn't need to be told to pass along the information to the six men behind him. He turned and relayed the information to Frank. He smelled the odor of sweat and garlic emanating from the man. Turning back, he tried to keep his heart beating at less than

71

100 beats per minute. Raising his rifle, he switched the safety lever to the burst fire position. He could not even see his front sight.

Sitting on his right leg, Lucas braced his left elbow on the inside of his left knee, pointing his rifle at the ten o'clock coordinate. *Damn. They don't train us for this.*

Every sound in the jungle seemed amplified. The insects sounded like buzz saws. Lucas could hear the gurgling of a river that must have been miles away. His throat was parched. He wanted to drink some water and needed to urinate, but he remained motionless.

He heard a pop followed by a sizzle, the sound moving upwards. Suddenly a bright light exploded overhead, lighting up the jungle all around. Raising his rear sights, he pointed toward a group of men who were carrying large bundles on their backs. Vega's team opened fire on them.

Lucas picked out a man who was crouching and running to the right. Lining up his front sight on the man's torso, Lucas pressed the trigger. He watched the man stop, fall over to his left, and then stop moving altogether. Lucas watched the body for a few seconds and then tried to acquire a new target.

There was only one man left standing. The man in the front of the fallen bodies dropped his rifle, raising his hands in surrender. He stood there, looking around in fear. Lucas saw a muzzle flash from far ahead, and the man's head disappeared in a cloud of pink mist.

The soldiers in Vega's team turned on their flashlights and head lamps and moved toward the group of now dead bodies. Holstein turned on his flashlight and started down the hill as well.
Lucas turned on his headlamp, as did the men behind him. They all converged on the site of the massacre.

Vega's men got there first, and made certain no one was still alive. Lucas arrived a few steps behind Holstein. Vega was laughing and clapping his men on their shoulders. Lucas noticed that ten of Vega's men were not wearing backpacks. He wondered if they had dropped them back on the trail. His question was soon answered, as the ten men pulled the bundles off of the dead men and heaved them on their backs.

Vega walked over to Holstein and shook his meaty hand. "Tonight was a very successful operation. We put a major dent in the cartel's business. I thank you, and I thank your men."

Holstein shook Vega's hand, but did not return the smile.

***

Back at the camp, Lucas found Holstein sitting alone in front of one of the smaller campfires. The Americans and the Jungle Brigade soldiers were whooping it up around a large bonfire near the kitchen. Bottles of wine were being passed around. Lucas spotted Vega in the mess tent, talking on a radio.

"Mind if I join you, Jake?"

"Pull up a log."

Lucas found a small tree stump and rolled it over next to Jake. He adjusted his sidearm and sitting down, he stared at the fire and began to lose himself in the crackling flames. They watched the fire in silence for several minutes.

Clearing his throat, Jake said, "Lucas? What do you think about what happened today."

Thinking a few moments before replying, he said, "There is something about Vega that makes me uncomfortable. When I first met him and he shook my hand, I felt a surge of anger in my gut. At first, I thought it was because I thought you set me up with that fake argument at the airport. Later, I watched him talking to you and the men, and there was something off. He seemed too hospitable. His humor seemed cold underneath."

"Yeah. What else?"

Lucas thought for a few moments. "Then when we ambushed those guys in the jungle, he seemed to take pleasure in the massacre. It also seemed like he also planned ahead of time to confiscate the bundles of drugs, and he knew precisely how many men he needed to carry them back here."

Holstein nodded. "As you know, this is supposed to be a joint operation. They call it Operation Genesis. But, he's not telling me how he gets the intel. When I asked him what he was going to do with the drugs, he just laughed, and said they were going to be put into the evidence storage center back at Posadas."

Jake picked up a stick and moved a few logs around in the fire. A burst of embers rose into the sky. "What did you mean about anger in your gut?'

Lucas sighed. "Back when I was doing forensic work, and then later in Panama, I sometimes had the same feeling in my gut when interviewing certain people."

"What do you mean? What kind of people?"

Lucas turned and looked Jake in the eye. "The only ones that triggered that feeling, each and every one, turned out to be what we used to call psychopaths."

"Psychopaths? You mean crazy killers?"

"No. They were not crazy. At least not crazy like you may be thinking. No, psychopaths are people who are wired differently than the rest of us. They typically have little or no fear. They also have no empathy for others. They enjoy manipulating people and are often very good at it. They read people to exploit their weaknesses."

Jake nodded, staring into the fire.

Lucas continued, "They also see themselves as superior to normal people. They think our feelings of love and compassion are signs of weakness. In particular, they think that rules and laws do not apply to them. Many of them become successful criminals. Some become successful salesman." After a moment, Lucas added, "Or even politicians."

Lucas thought for a moment. "I don't know why, but when I talk to a psychopath, or listen to them talking to others, my gut twists inside."

"And you got that feeling around Vega?"

"I'm sorry, Jake. I know he's your friend. But, I think you need to be very careful around him."

A noise from behind him snapped him back to the present. A group of men in black fatigues were now moving cautiously into the camp from behind the barracks tents. Lucas dropped down into a prone position while pulling his sidearm from his holster. Aiming at the men, he remembered that his rifle was in the barracks tent, twenty feet away.

He sensed that Holstein had also dropped prone. The invaders were coming in from several directions. Lucas looked over his shoulder and saw another group coming in from behind the kitchen. Switching his focus to the mess tent, he saw that Vega was gone.

Searching the ground around him, he found a baseball sized rock. Transferring his sidearm to his support hand, he grabbed the rock. Rising up to his knees, he spotted Frank and threw the rock at his torso. The rock bounced off of Frank's hip. Frank let out a yelp and spun around, searching for whomever threw it. His hand reflexively grabbed the grip of his sidearm. He spotted Lucas waving for him to get down.

The invaders opened fire from the barracks. Holstein started to return fire, taking out two of the invaders in quick succession, with two rounds to the chest each. Lucas fired two rounds into the center mass of a third invader. As the man fell, Jake and Holstein rolled to the left. Lucas transferred his gun to his right hand and fired two more rounds, catching another invader in the neck and face.

The invaders from the kitchen opened up on the soldiers around the bonfire. Ten of the soldiers dropped dead within seconds, riddled with bullets. Frank was crouching low and running away from the bonfire, his pistol firing into the invaders behind him. Bullets were striking the dirt around his feet, following him into the darkness.

Lucas jumped to his feet and started running to the barracks, trying to keep the tent between him and the invaders as concealment. Several of the soldiers had pulled out their side arms and tried to return fire as they scattered. Four more of them were shot even before they could start running.

Lucas reached the tent just as an invader rounded the corner, his rifle aimed at Lucas' head. Lucas tried to raise his pistol, knowing it was too late. Time slowed as Lucas looked into the man's brown eyes. The man was young, almost still a boy. The right side of the man's head exploded as he fell behind the tent. Lucas watched him fall in slow motion.

Turning to his right, he locked eyes with Jake. Jake just nodded, as he rolled again and took aim at another invader.

Leaping into the tent, Lucas found his rifle and grabbed his pack, slipping into the straps. He holstered his sidearm, and grabbed another rifle. He quickly checked the chambers and magazines. Both rifles were ready for action.

Stealthily moving to the back of the tent, he carefully stuck his head under the sidewall. There were no invaders in front of him, but he could see eight or nine of them to his right. Slipping outside, he rolled into a kneeling position and raised the rifle's sights. Flipping the safety to full auto, he fired a long burst, raking back and forth. He dropped half of them before they turned and started returning fire. He was already gone, having run ten yards to the left, behind a tree. He inserted a fresh magazine.

Switching to burst mode, he stood and fired, taking out two more invaders before running back behind the tent. Crouching low, he felt incoming bullets tearing through the tent fabric inches above his head.

Lucas kept moving until he reached the end of the tent. He performed a tactical reload, slipping the partially empty magazine into a side pouch and inserting a fresh magazine into the rifle. Raising his sights, he leaned out and saw three more invaders heading his way.

Jake was still on the ground, firing at one of them. Lucas saw the slide lock back on Jake's pistol. He was empty.

The three invaders stopped and took aim at Jake. They were too far apart for Lucas to get all three. He fired a burst at the closet one, dropping him instantly. He took aim at the second one as the man turned toward him and fired back. Lucas felt a hot poker stick in his right side, spinning him around behind the tent.

Falling to his knees, he dropped down into a prone position, his front sight covering the man's chest. The pain in his side was excruciating. Pressing the trigger, he watched as the man fell backward. The third man was pointing at his head. Lucas heard Jake screaming his name. Lucas heard a gunshot come from the left, and saw the man's face disappear.

Lucas looked at Jake, but both of his hands were on the ground, one of them still gripping his empty pistol. Lucas forced himself to get up and he stumbled to Jake's side, handing him one of the rifles. Falling into a prone position, Lucas tried to aim at the invaders at the kitchen, who were killing the last of the soldiers.

Jake took the rifle and ran in a low crouch far to the right, dropping down into prone and aiming at the remaining invaders. Lucas and Jake both opened fire at the same second.

Lucas thought he saw at least ten men, and managed to drop four of them. Jake took out another three. The remaining invaders returned fire as they retreated behind the kitchen.

Jake was up and running, trying to flank them from the right. Lucas struggled to get up and started to run to the left, but the searing pain from his side caused him to drop to the ground. Grunting, he rolled into a prone position and lifted his sights toward the kitchen. He heard Jake fire several bursts and heard a man scream in pain.

Lucas saw a man peak his head out from the left of the kitchen, but then pull back. He took aim at the tent wall where he thought the man might be, and let out two bursts. He heard the man scream as he fell next to the tent. *Only one more left, I hope.*

Lucas kept his sights on the kitchen, but his vision was starting to blur. Jake was in the open, and bullets were hitting the ground in front of him. Jake tried to roll out of the way, but the bullets followed him, getting closer.

Lucas heard a loud bang, and the firing stopped. He tried to stand, getting up on his knees, but dizzy from the loss of blood he fell over. He was staring at the fire and then there was darkness.

***

Yelling. More yelling. Who is yelling my name? Dad? Dad? Is that you?

There was only blackness. Then, it started again.

"Lucas. Lucas. Wake up, you bastard."

He felt a hard slap across his cheek. He reached for his pistol, but found an empty holster.

"He's coming around. Lucas, wake up."

Lucas thought he recognized the voice. He smelled garlic. Slowly he opened his right eye. A big blue eye was staring at him from inches away. The face was contorted in anger. The mouth opened and started yelling his name again, "Lucas. Wake the fuck up."

Both of his eyes popped open as he reflexively raised his fists to fight off an attacker. Something stabbed him in the side, and he screamed in pain.

A distorted voice said, "Whoa, buddy. Lie still. You're wounded, but you're safe now, buddy."

Lucas groaned as he tried to focus. There were two faces now. Ugly, dirty faces. *Oh no. I'm in hell. Oh no. Lord, I'm sorry, please forgive me.*

"What the hell is he mumbling about?" Jake asked.

"Shit, I don't know. He's delirious or something."

Lucas finally recognized the voice, and the smell of garlic. His eyes came into focus, and he was staring into Frank's worried face.

"Frank. Buddy. What are you doing in hell?"

Frank laughed. He said, "Welcome back, Lucas. I'm sorry, but hell doesn't want you; At least not for a while."

Lucas started to laugh, but the pain in his side screamed at him to stop.

"What happened? Are you guys okay?"

Frank answered, "Yeah, we're fine. Thanks to you, you lunkhead. Thanks for hitting me with that rock."

What's he talking about? Then Lucas slowly remembered what had happened. "Oh yeah, the rock. I was aiming for your head. I guess I missed."

"You almost hit me in a worse place."

"Yes, well, I never was any good at baseball."

Jake chimed in. "Maybe, but you are a hell of a shot with firearms. You saved my life, asshole. Now, I have to owe you one."

Lucas tried to think back to the firefight. He felt confused. "But I couldn't stop the guy at the barracks." He thought a little more. "And, I passed out before I could get the guy at the kitchen."

Jake replied, "Yeah, well, you did your best. And, when your best wasn't good enough, Frank stepped in."

"Frank? That was you? You took out those guys?"

Frank looked down. "Well, I didn't want to have to walk out of here all by myself. So, I guess I saved your skinny ass." Looking at Jake, he added, "And I saved your big ass as well."

"That you did, son. I won't forget it."

"What about our guys?" Lucas asked.

Frank looked away. Jake answered, "Sorry, buddy. They didn't make it."

Lucas closed his eyes. He said a prayer for them all.

Frank shouted, "Lucas! Don't go away again."

Lucas opened his eyes. "I'm here. I'm here. What do we do now?"

Jake spelled it out. "Well, you got shot. I don't think any vital organs were hit, but you've lost a lot of blood. Frank managed to stop your bleeding. The bullet went right through you. You've got duct tape closing your wounds on both sides. Frank wrapped you up pretty good. We have plenty of ammo, food and water. The Jeeps and the trucks seem to be working." Jake looked away.

"What aren't you telling me?" Lucas asked.

Jake answered, "Vega is missing. His body isn't here."

"Yeah, well, I noticed he was missing before the shooting started. I'm thinking he called it in. I saw him on the radio. He wanted the drugs all to himself. He's a corrupt SOB."

Jake looked around. "Well, that means he is still out there. Who knows what we are going to run into on the way back to Posadas."

Frank asked, "Can't we call in for an evac?"

Shaking his head, Jake replied, "The only radios here are destroyed. We are on our own until we get back to

Posadas. Even then, we may still be on our own. There is no telling how deep the corruption runs."

Looking down at Lucas, he continued, "We have a long way back on a bumpy road. I'm sorry, but you're gonna be in a lot of pain. We don't have any morphine or pain killers."

"Wait, we have this." Frank reached into his pack and pulled out a bottle of Malbec.

Lucas smiled. "Don't tell anybody, but I love you, man."

***

Frank asked, "Can we go now?"

Jake looked around the camp. There were bodies everywhere.

"Frank, help me pick up all the firearms and load them into the truck."

It took them fifteen minutes to complete the task.

"Oh crap," Frank shouted from the kitchen. He was stomping around with his hands balled into fists, shaking them in the air.

Raising his rifle to the ready, Jake asked, "What's wrong?

"What's wrong? What's wrong? They killed all the Malbec."

Jake shook his head and turned away. He thought Frank might start crying.

Stepping out of the kitchen, Frank lowered his head and asked, "Are we ready to go now?"

Jake answered, "No. Now I need you to disable all of the vehicles except the truck. I don't want Vega coming back here to find anything useful."

Frank knew exactly what to do and it only took him another fifteen minutes to sabotage the vehicles. "Now can we go?"

Jake replied, "No. There is one more thing I have to do."

He walked back behind the kitchen tent. He emerged with a five gallon Jerry can and began pouring gasoline on top of the bundles of drugs. He ended by pouring a trail of gas from the pile of bundles to where Frank was standing.

Looking at Frank, he asked, "Well? Got a match?"

"Even better, I've got my trusty Zippo."

Frank reached into his jacket and pulled out a battered lighter. He kissed it once and flicked it open.

Kneeling down, he spun the wheel and lit the trail of gas. In a few seconds, the pile was in flames.

"That lighter mean something special to you?" Jake asked.

Flicking the lid open and shut a few times, Frank replied, "It was my Dad's. He said it got him through Okinawa."

Frank spent the next thirty minutes constructing a stretcher. He then climbed into the back of the truck and rigged up a sling with bungee cords to cushion the bumps in the road. They moved Lucas onto the stretcher, and then lifted him into the contraption in back of the truck.

Frank said, "You might get seasick, but at least the bumps won't be so bad."

Frank and Jake finished loading the truck with several crates, ammunition and a few more rifles. Frank picked one up and checked the magazine and the chamber. Handling the rifle to Lucas, he said, "Lock and load. Safety's on." He did the same with a pistol, slipping it into Lucas' holster.

Reaching into his pack, Frank pulled out the last bottle of wine. Using his multitool, he removed the cork. "If you need anything else, just yell out."

"Thanks, Frank." Holding up the bottle, Lucas said, "Cheers."

Frank and Jake climbed into the cab, with Frank driving, and started back to Posadas. It took them two hours to get back to the edge of civilization. Frank pulled over under the cover of some trees to check on Lucas. He started to get out of the truck, but stopped when he heard the sound of a helicopter coming from back up the road.

A black helicopter passed overhead, heading toward Posadas. After it was gone, Frank jumped out.

Climbing into the back of the truck, Frank stopped. His blood ran cold. Lucas was gone.

Chapter 8

The Abduction

Writhing in pain, Lucas was in agony. The truck had been rolling for less than half an hour. The sling that Frank had constructed worked great, by cushioning the bumps in the road, but the swinging kept putting pressure on his wound. The bottle of wine was now empty, but the fragrant garnet-colored fluid barely took the edge off of his misery.

His head was swimming and he could barely keep his eyes open. *Maybe I should just give in and go to sleep.* Closing his eyes, finally succumbing to the wine, Lucas passed out in minutes.

Three men in dirty brown robes watched from a distance, as the truck lumbered down the dirt track toward them. The taller one pulled out a radio and spoke briefly into it. Lifting it to his ear, he listened and nodded.

Turning to the other two, he said, "The one we want is in the back of the truck."

Silently moving through the jungle, the men worked their way down to a sharp bend in the road. They knew the truck would be forced to slow down at this point. Hiding behind the thick undergrowth, the three men waited patiently.

Jake busied himself scanning the trees and bushes ahead, occasionally turning around to look out the window, making sure they weren't being followed. Frank's eyes were glued to the road ten feet in front of the truck, constantly making corrections, steering around the larger holes in the dirt road. Every few seconds, he wiped his face on his sleeve as his sweat kept running into his eyes.

As they approached a sharp turn to the left, Frank said, "I've got to slow down here." Reaching down, he slammed the truck into a lower gear. Jake stuck his head out of the window, bringing his rifle to the ready. Using his camo print bandana, he wiped the sweat from his eyes. The truck lurched over two large partially buried boulders in the dirt. The barrel of the rifle banged against the window frame.

As soon as the truck passed them, the three robed men rolled out of the bushes and grabbed on to the tailgate. Swinging their bodies over the gate, they landed softly onto the truck bed, crouching down immediately. They froze into position, facing forward, and one man keeping watch behind them.

The taller man moved forward silently, keeping his eyes on the man lying in a sling. Reaching into his pouch, he removed a bottle of clear liquid and a thick cloth. Pouring some of the liquid onto the cloth, he closed the bottle and slipped it back into his pouch. Reaching out, he softly placed the damp cloth over the sleeping man's mouth and nose.

Lucas stirred briefly and groaned. His eyes never opened. The tall man wrapped a bandana over the cloth and tied it loosely, holding the cloth in place.

The tall man whispered to his companions, "Now."

One of the men joined him and they lifted the stretcher, with Lucas on it, out of the sling. The third man straddled the tailgate. They brought Lucas' body to the back of the truck passing one end of the stretcher to the man on the tailgate, while the other man held on to the other end. The tall man swung himself down to the road, now jogging slightly to keep up with the truck. The two men passed one end of the stretcher down to him, and then they too jumped out of the truck. As the truck rounded the corner, the three men with the stretcher had already disappeared into the undergrowth.

The men waited patiently. No one spoke. Lucas remained motionless on the stretcher. The tall man lifted Lucas' bloodied shirt and examined the duct tape wrappings. Shaking his head he took the wrist of the unconscious Lucas, checking his pulse. Moving to his head, he lifted Lucas' eyelids and examined his eyes. Lucas never stirred. The tall man spent a few more minutes checking for other wounds, but found nothing troublesome. He removed the firearm from Lucas' holster, and stuffed it into his pouch.

Hearing the sound of an engine, the tall man stood up slowly, looking back up the road. A battered green pickup truck soon appeared, driven by an old man wearing an identical brown robe. The tall man waved him down and the truck stopped next to them, idling roughly. The three men lifted the stretcher into the back of the pickup, two of the men remaining in the back, while the tall man climbed into the passenger side.

The old man worked the gear shift until he found reverse. He backed up, turning the wheel until the back of the pickup pushed into the bushes. Reversing the wheel and shifting into first gear, the truck then headed back up the road. The old man croaked, "Is he okay?"

The tall man said, "He will be."

They drove a few miles up the road, stopping where the undergrowth of the jungle was the thickest. The two men in the back jumped out, and moving forward, they grabbed opposite ends of a large bush. Pulling the bush out in front of the pickup, a faint two track road appeared to the left. The old man turned the truck onto the hidden road, stopping after twenty feet. The two men pulled the bush back into position, concealing the entrance once again. They hopped back into the bed of the pickup as the old man started rolling forward.

***

Lucas slowly started regaining consciousness. Before opening his eyes, he noticed that the swinging had stopped and he could not hear the truck engine. The pain in his side had diminished drastically to a dull throbbing. Straining his ears, he listened for the sounds of his companions. Only the buzz saw racket of insects and the calling of a few distant birds could be heard. Lucas tried to keep his breathing steady. He sensed that something was amiss. Somehow, he was no longer in the truck. *Maybe I'm in a hospital.* But, it didn't smell like a hospital. It still smelled like the jungle.

As slowly as possible, he began opening his left eye. There was a wooden ceiling above his body. Rolling his eye to the left, then down, and then to the right, he could see no sign of anyone else. Closing his left eye, he slowly opened his right eye. Still no one was within his limited vision. Feeling slightly more secure, he fully opened both eyes. He was inside some kind of wooden structure. Trying to sit up, the pain in his side increased, but it was still tolerable. He quickly scanned his surroundings. He was alone in a large room.

Standing up, his head throbbed as he fought off the sensation of passing out. Reaching out with his left arm, he steadied himself against a wall made of interlaced wooden panels. On his right was a table with a few medical instruments and many bottles containing liquids and dried materials. Turning around, he saw several empty beds. The room was only about 12 feet by 12 feet. Looking down, he saw the floor consisted of hard packed clay.

His shirt and pants were gone, and he was wearing a long sleeved brown robe. His pistol and rifle were gone. Reaching across to the table, he found something that resembled a scalpel, and picked it up. Checking around his robe, he noticed there were no pockets. Spotting a piece of tubing on the table, Lucas wrapped the tubing around his left forearm and tied it off. He slipped the scalpel between the tubing and his skin. Shaking his arm a few times, he was satisfied that it wouldn't drop out of the makeshift sheath.

Lifting up his robe, he checked his wounds. The duct tape was gone, and it had been replaced with gauze and white tape. Feeling around his lower back, he felt a similar bandage. There was no blood on his front side bandage, and the rear bandage also felt dry. Applying pressure on the wound did not result in the pain he expected. The same was true for his exit wound. *How long have I been unconscious? It feels almost healed.*

Hearing voices and footsteps, Lucas sat down on his bed and waited.

The handle on the door started turning, and the door opened inward. Standing in the doorway was a very old man with gray hair down to his shoulders. He was wearing a brown robe identical to the one Lucas was wearing. The old man's skin was tanned, but he was definitely not a native Latino. He sported a neatly trimmed beard and his blue eyes widened when he saw Lucas sitting up. Taking a few steps into the room, he closed the door behind him.

"Ah, I see you have finally come back to us. The man spoke English with a vaguely German accent. "I assume you speak English, yes?"

Lucas only nodded.

"Well then. How are you feeling?" He looked genuinely concerned.

Lucas replied, "I've been better."

"Yes, yes. You are in magnificent shape. But your wounds were serious. They had become infected, and you had lost a lot of blood. We replenished your fluids and cured the infection."

"How long was I unconscious?"

"My companions picked you up almost three weeks ago and brought you here."

Lucas shook his head, letting that sink in. *Three weeks*. "Where are my companions?"

"I am afraid I do not have that information." Seeing the tension in Lucas' face, the old man continued. "We did nothing to harm them. We only brought you here."

"Why am I here? Who the hell is 'we', and who the hell are you?" Lucas asked.

"Oh yes, please forgive my manners. My name is Hanz Schwartz. I am the appointed leader of our little group." The old man reached out with his bony wrinkled hand.

Lucas just stared into the man's eyes, ignoring his outstretched hand.

Hanz seemed genuinely saddened. Withdrawing his hand slowly, Hanz continued. "We are, what you might call, healers. I trust you noticed that you are healing quite well?"

Ignoring the question, Lucas asked, "You have given me your name, but you still haven't answered my question. Why am I here?"

Hanz nodded and replied, "Yes, of course. I am afraid that is a rather long story. Perhaps you will join me for dinner and I will attempt to answer all of your questions. I imagine you are quite hungry."

Lucas hadn't noticed until Hanz brought it up, but he really was famished.

Hanz said, "I will send for you in about thirty minutes, jungle time." He smiled with brilliant white teeth, and there was a twinkle in his eye. "Dinner jackets are not required." Turning around, he left the room without another word, closing the door behind him.

Lucas stood up, ignoring the dizziness, and went to the door. Turning the handle, he opened the door a crack and peered out. It was getting dark outside, but he could see the old man walking vigorously across an open courtyard toward a large two-story stone building, several hundred feet away. Four men in brown robes were moving around the building. Some were carrying bundles, while others had what appeared to be hoes and rakes. No one was armed.

Lucas closed the door and returned to the table. He searched for something potentially useful, but found nothing. Returning to the door, he opened it slowly and slipped outside. To his right he saw a battered green pickup truck sitting at the end of a two track road. The road disappeared into thick jungle. The building he just left backed up to more jungle. The only open area was between his building and the large stone building.

Crouching low, he moved into the jungle to his left. Moving slowly, mostly because of the thickness of the foliage, he tried to make his way to the back of the stone structure. He worried about encountering snakes or other poisonous creatures, so he stepped carefully while looking all around. Moving forward, ten steps at a time, he then stopped and listened before moving again. Soon, he passed the stone structure to his right, and searched the small open area behind the building. He heard a generator humming, but could not see it from his position. The building was surrounded by dense jungle.

Lucas waited a few minutes to see if any more robed men were in the area. He spotted two windows with a wooden door between them. Seeing no movement, and staying as low as he could, he moved quickly to the back of the structure. He could hear muffled voices from inside the building, but could not make out what they were saying.

Rising up to the edge of the window, he tried to look inside. All he could see was darkness, and vague outlines of furniture. It appeared to be a bedroom with several bunk beds. Moving to the edge of the second window, he sneaked a look inside. It appeared to have the same furniture and bunk beds.

Crouching down again, he moved to the edge of the building and peered around the corner. A large yellow diesel generator was chugging along, pumping gray exhaust into the air. A large cylindrical tank was on the far side, and there were white PVC pipes leading from the tank, into the building. He assumed it was a water tank or cistern. To the left was a large pile of refuse, contained inside of a wooden bin made of wood and chicken wire. It appeared to be only organic waste, as he could see no plastic or pieces of metal. He could see a small wooden structure, behind the pile, that looked like an outhouse.

Satisfied that there was nothing of concern, he made his way back through the jungle toward his room. When he reached his building, he scanned the courtyard and saw that all of the robed men were gone. He slipped back inside and waited, sitting on the bed.

Ten minutes later, he heard a soft knock on the door and a young man entered, carrying a lantern. He was wearing the same brown robe. His long black hair was pulled back and tied with a small rope. His hair hung down past his waist. The man had the facial structure of an indigenous native. He did not speak, nor did he smile, but he beckoned Lucas to come with him, and walked outside. Lucas stood up and followed him. He did not feel dizzy this time.

He followed the young man to the stone building. It was now dark outside, and the lantern cast eerie shadows on the ground. Arriving at the building, the man opened the door and waived Lucas inside. After doing a quick scan of the interior, Lucas entered. To the left was a stone dividing wall with a closed door in the middle. A hallway continued straight ahead. To the right was a large open room. Five men of varying ages were sitting at a long wooden table. Three lanterns hung overhead. Hanz was at the head of the table, speaking to the man to his right. The men all appeared to be of the same indigenous origins as his escort. Lucas and Hanz were the only Anglos.

When Hanz noticed Lucas, he stood up and waved him forward. The men at the table all turned around to look at him. Their expressions were blank, but slightly curious. There were two empty chairs, and Hanz pointed Lucas to the one opposite his own chair. Lucas saw an open door behind Hanz, and assumed that it passed into a kitchen. He walked forward, keeping his eyes on the men, pulled out his chair, and sat down. His escort took the remaining empty chair to his left, as Hanz sat down.

The man to his right passed him a large glass pitcher filled with a clear liquid. Lucas took the pitcher and filled his glass. Hanz raised his glass and took a drink, keeping his eyes on Lucas. Lucas watched as one of the other men took a drink from a glass. Lucas raised his own glass and sniffed it, noting that it had no odor. Taking a small sip, he found that it was likely just water. Realizing that he was parched, he downed the contents, and poured himself a second full glass.

Hanz spoke first, "Thank you for coming. I hope you enjoy our humble offerings." He repeated himself in fluent Spanish to the other men.

Lucas raised his glass towards Hanz and nodded affirmatively.

A man entered from the kitchen, carrying a tray with a bowl of bread and another bowl of salad. He set it down in front of Hanz, and returned to the kitchen. Lucas thought he smelled meat cooking, and his stomach growled in anticipation.

Hanz stood up and picked up the round loaf of bread. He raised it up over his head and closed his eyes. The men all bowed their heads.

"Heavenly Father, we thank you for this food. Bless those who planted and harvested the grain. Bless those who milled the grain for us, and made it bread. May it nourish us and heal us." He then repeated the same blessing in Spanish.

Hanz sat down and tore off a chuck of bread before passing it to his right. While the bread was being passed around, Hanz put some salad on his plate, then passing the bowl to his right. Lucas took the same sized portion of bread and salad as the others, resisting the urge to keep it all to himself, and passed it along.

He swallowed the bread in three gulps and dug into the salad. When he finished the salad he reached for his glass, looking up. The men were all wide-eyed, staring at him. Their bread and salads were untouched.

Hanz said in Spanish, "It is okay. He is very hungry."

The man from the kitchen returned with a large steaming cast iron pot and set it down in front of Hanz. Hanz stood up and lifted up the heavy pot in front of him. Closing his eyes again, he spoke another blessing, first in English and then in Spanish. He then ladled a portion of the stew onto his plate. The men began passing their plates to Hanz as he spooned large servings on to each one. Lucas smiled weakly and shrugged, passing his plate forward.

The stew was delicious. Lucas tasted beef, seasoned with onions, peppers, cilantro and several mysterious spices. He finished before anyone else, and waited, sipping his water as he watched the others eat slowly. They closed their eyes while chewing each mouthful. It seemed like they took forever to finish.

When they finished, Hanz spoke directly to Lucas. "I would offer you a second serving, but your body is not yet accustomed to solid food. There will be plenty tomorrow to satisfy your hunger."

Lucas nodded, reluctantly agreeing with the old man. "Thank you. I am most grateful for sharing your food with me."

Hanz stood up, and the men also rose. The men filed out of the room and proceeded down the hallway. They disappeared into the rooms at the back of the building.

Hanz came around the table and said, "Please join me in my study." Without waiting for a response, he walked over to the door in the stone wall and opened it, looking expectantly at Lucas. Wanting some answers, Lucas followed and entered the room.

Chapter 9

Brujos

Hanz' study was Spartan. There were four straight-backed wooden chairs, a small wooden desk with a kerosene lamp, and a bookshelf containing at most, thirty books. A table next to the desk was piled with paper manuscripts. A map of South America hung on one wall, and there were a dozen or more red pins marking various locations. A second map, of Central and North America, hung on another wall, and it too had a number of red pins sticking out of it. In one corner, stood a wooden reading stand that held a large open book.

Hanz motioned Lucas to one of the chairs. Once seated, Lucas watched Hanz pull up another chair, and he then sat down facing Lucas.

Hanz studied Lucas' face for a few moments before he began speaking.

"As I said earlier, my name is Hanz Schwartz. I am originally from, what later came to be known as West Germany. I was born in 1925 in a small village named Passau, near the borders of Austria and Czechoslovakia. I was drafted into the German Army when I was 17 years old, under the rule of that evil creature, Adolf Hitler. I served one year before escaping into Switzerland. I then worked for the resistance until the end of the war."

Hanz stared at a blank wall for a minute before continuing. "After the war, I was hired by British intelligence to assist in spying against the Russians. In 1946, I was sent to Buenos Aires to assist in tracking down Nazi war criminals. In August, 1947, I was suddenly assigned to a secret mission to, how do you say it? Stowaway?

Lucas nodded.

"Yes, stowaway. I was to stowaway, onboard an airplane bound for Santiago, Chile. It was thought that one of the passengers was carrying Nazi documents that were important, because they contained the names of several war criminals in Argentina. I had a code word assigned to the mission, and I was supposed to transmit the word over the radio once I had the documents in my possession."

Hanz stood and walked over to the map of South America. His finger traced a route from Buenos Aires to the Andes. "I still remember that plane. It was a Lancastrian Star Dust, two engines. Toward the end of the flight, I emerged from my hiding place. I had a pistol, and I found the man who was carrying the documents. I pointed my gun at the man, but suddenly the plane hit some turbulence and I was thrown off balance. My pistol discharged and I shot the pilot by mistake."

He pointed to a spot on the map. "It must have been right here. The man and I fought for a minute and my pistol discharged two more times. The bullets must have hit something important, because the plane started smoking and one of the engines caught on fire. I finally was able to knock the man out and obtained his briefcase."

I thought I was going to die. I yelled at the radio operator, telling him I was working for British intelligence and I had to get a message out over the radio. It was my code word."

Lucas sat forward in his chair. "What happened?"

"I told him to send the code word, all initials. They typed messages over the radios in those days. The coded message was STNDOC, which simply stood for 'Secured The Nazi Documents'. The radio operator sent the message, but I later learned that he misspelled what I had told him. The message he sent was 'STENDEC'. The airplane was now on fire, but I was wearing a parachute. I ran to the back of the plane and jumped out."

Hanz paused for a moment, overcome with emotion. "I felt like a coward, leaving all those poor people behind. But, I had to get those documents into the hands of British intelligence."

Hanz hung his head, pulling himself together. Lucas waited patiently for him to continue.

"My parachute opened, but it was so cold, that I dropped the briefcase. I was at such a high altitude that I hit the ground at such great speed, I broke my leg and passed out."

Hanz walked slowly back to his chair and sat down. He stared at his feet for another minute before he could speak.

"I awakened inside a metal room. I was in excruciating pain from my broken leg. There were four men leaning over me. They were speaking in a language that I could not understand. They stood up and started singing. I thought I was delirious, or maybe I was in hell. The metal room started vibrating and the walls turned many different colors. I felt myself vibrating and suddenly, the pain in my leg started to go away. But then I passed out again."

Hanz looked up at Lucas, who was staring at him incredulously.

"I know. I know it sounds crazy. I thought I must be crazy. I thought maybe I hit my head too hard. When I awakened again, the four men were sitting at my feet with their eyes closed. I sat up, and my leg was no longer hurting. I felt it with my hands, and it was no longer broken."

Hanz looked at Lucas with pleading eyes. "It was no longer broken. How could that be?"

Lucas answered, "I do not know. Are you sure it had been broken?"

"Yes. Yes it was broken. It was bent at a wrong angle. I had seen such breaks before, when I was in the army. I am certain it was broken, but then there it was, somehow, healed."

"What did you do?"

I didn't know what to do. I spoke to them in German. I then tried English. They just looked at me quizzically. I then tried Spanish, and one of the men understood me. He told me that we were in a very special place. He said the gods built this room. He told me that I was the first god that he had seen."

"He thought you were a god?"

"Yes. He said I fell out of the sky, so I must be a god. He spoke to the other men, and they all bowed down to me."

Hanz continued. "He said that they all saw a great fire eagle flying through the night sky. They then saw that it plowed into the mountain side, and then they saw it set itself on fire. It caused a large avalanche. Then they saw me falling from the heavens. They saw that I was white skinned and had blonde hair. They had never seen a white man before. They were afraid because I was unconscious, so they brought me to the holy room of the gods. They called it Arcum Deus.

They sang an ancient song taught to them by their Brujos, and I was healed."

"Brujos? You mean sorcerers?"

"Yes. They were all Brujos: Sorcerers who practiced ancient magic and healing ceremonies."

Lucas sat back in his chair and tried to analyze everything Hanz had told him. He thought Hanz might be delusional, but he did not come across as psychotic. He seemed rational enough, except for this fantastic story,

Hanz continued. "Because my skin was white, they said I must be a Brujo Blanco, a white sorcerer god, who practiced white magic, good magic. Magic that heals people. They thanked me for coming to them when they were in a life and death struggle with practitioners of black magic, evil magic. They knew I was sent here to save them."

Lucas said, "I am guessing you decided to go along with it. You didn't tell them the truth?"

Hanz looked down at his feet. He said, "Maybe it was wrong. I was a weak man. But, I had seen such evil in the world. I saw firsthand the evil of Hitler and Nazism. I saw the evil of communism. I thought that maybe this room, the room of the gods, as he called it; maybe this room had power to overcome evil in the world."

"And what? You thought you could harness the power of this room and save the world?

"I didn't know what to think. All I knew was that something about this room could heal me. It healed my broken leg. I thought maybe this really was a room of the gods. Maybe their gods brought me there to do some good in the world. There were eleven people onboard that plane, and they all died because of me. I thought I owed them something."

"So, you let them think you were a god, a white Brujo god?"

"What would you have done?" Hanz asked. "Yes. I let them think I was a god. I then told them that I was going to test them. They had to teach me everything they knew. I told them that I would know if they were lying, and I would know if they left anything out. I told them that they would die horrible deaths if they tried to fool me."

Hanz continued. There was a wild look in his eyes. "We spent many months in that Arcum Deus. One of the men would leave and come back with food and supplies. Soon, others would show up and bow down to me, and bring me gold and diamonds. They brought parts of the airplane they had found in the ice. I learned all of their secrets. I learned that there was a special doorway in the room that could transport objects, and even people from one place to another. I learned that there were special rooms, just like that one, all over the world."

Hanz stood up and walked to the maps, his face reflecting intensity as he continued. "Do you see these red pins? Each one shows where these special rooms are. I can travel from one spot to another almost instantaneously. Each room is attached to a volcano, hidden within lava tubes."

Lucas' head was spinning. He began to think the old man really was insane. Maybe Hanz did hit his head too hard, and this delusional story of his must be the result of some brain trauma. Lucas had interviewed a number of inmates who had delusions. Yet, none of the inmates' delusions were as detailed as the old man's. This was different. *What if he is telling the truth?*

Hanz pressed on. "In the months that followed, we started to go out of the room and into the villages. They offered me young women. When they later became pregnant, the women would be honored, and their children would be revered. I went from village to village, and the people all bowed down to me and gave me precious gifts. I developed a group of trusted acolytes who took care of all of my needs."

Hanz sat down again, catching his breath.

After a few moments, Lucas asked, "What about the practioners of black magic that you mentioned?"

"Ah yes. They are called Brujos Negro, or Negros, depending on the dialect. They are sorcerers of the black arts. These are evil men and women. They prey upon the weak. They make and sell potions to do evil things, to hurt and kill others. They do not have any real magic though. They do not know about the special rooms. We have hidden that secret from them. The Brujos Blanco are dedicated to protecting and healing the people. The Brujo Negro want to exploit them. But, they are getting more powerful every day. Many young people are attracted to them, so their numbers are growing. Our numbers are diminishing. Very few young people seem interested in white magic. Many are already corrupted by the potions of the Brujos Negro."

Lucas thought deeply about their conversation. Standing up, he walked over to the maps. He noticed that there were no pins anywhere near Posadas.

Lucas asked, "So, what are you doing here, assuming we are still near Posadas? There are no red pins around here. "

"This is one of our northeastern outposts. The Brujos Negro are highly active here. They are manufacturing and distributing their evil drugs out of this area into Paraguay and northward. I came to try to stop what they are doing, but I do not have enough men."

"So, you kidnapped me to see if I would help you?"

"I am sorry that it seems like I kidnapped you. We were watching you and your team as soon as you landed. We have been watching your friend, Jake

Holstein, for a year. He is a good man, but he is not you.'

Lucas felt an uneasy feeling in his stomach. *Here it comes. Probably some bullshit con game.*

"What do you mean?" he asked.

"I am an old man. I cannot keep leading my people for much longer. I have been looking for someone to take over. You do not know this, but I met your father 25 years ago when he visited Mendoza. We became friends, and we kept in touch with each other over the years. He talked about you often. I have followed your career."

Hanz walked over to the book stand in the corner. He picked up the book and handed it to Lucas.

The title on the cover was a name: Lucas Forge.

.

Chapter 10

Posadas

Jake Holstein stood at attention in front of the Director's desk. He'd rather be dodging bullets in the jungle, than standing in this room. He wanted to be anywhere else but here.

Standing up, Director Triana slammed a file onto his desk.

"A disaster; that's all it is, a damned, unmitigated disaster." His face was red with anger. A vein pulsed across his forehead. "In all my years at this agency, I've never seen such a cluster fuck. Ten men, ten good men slaughtered. Jesus H Christ, Holstein."

The Director paced back and forth behind his desk, clenching and unclenching his fists. "Then you tell me that you lost Forge? You had him in the back of the truck and what, he just disappeared? A drunk, severely wounded agent, he just gets up and jumps out of the truck? He vanishes into thin air?"

The Director stopped pacing and placed his palms on the desk, leaning forward. "I had to send another team down there to clean up your mess. I had to pay big money to bribe the government officials to give us clearance to fly in a couple of helos to retrieve the bodies. Bodies that you should not have left behind." Raising his voice even louder, he said, "We. Don't. Leave. Soldiers. Behind."

"Yes sir, I mean, no sir." Holstein replied.

"Then, you let that corrupt asshole, Vega, your supposed friend, disappear too?"

"Sir, we had to get Forge to a hospital. There was no time to hunt for Vega, in the jungle that he knows. I thought he was on our side."

The Director stared at Holstein. "Holstein, nobody is on our side. Everybody is on the side of money. You should know that. I should send your ass back there, alone, to find Forge. Hell, Vega probably kidnapped him, right from under your nose. The whole operation in South America could be compromised."

"But sir, Lucas wouldn't talk. I know him," Jake said.

"You know him? Just like you know Vega? For all I know, they were in it together."

Holstein tensed up. His jaw muscles were pulsing. He wanted to strangle the Director for saying that.

The Director's eyes narrowed. "I know what you're thinking, Holstein. Go ahead and try it."

Jake stared at a spot on the wall and tried to calm himself. The Director sat down and steepled his fingers in front of his nose.

"I have to assume that our operations down there are blown and our agents are in danger. I have to reassign them and start over with a new batch of agents. Years of work just got flushed down the toilet, thanks to you."

Jake thought quickly. "Maybe not, sir."

"What do you mean, maybe not?"

Jake continued, "Sir, all I know, sir, is that Vega disappeared before the shooting started. Maybe he doesn't know that we figured it out. I could go back down there, and maybe I could find him. If I do, I can pretend that I am glad to see him unharmed. Maybe I can convince him that we don't know who attacked us, and tell him we think it was a rival cartel. Maybe I can find out if he knows what happened to Lucas."

Spinning his chair to the left, the Director looked out his window. The trees were swaying in the breeze. "That's a lot of 'maybes', Holstein."

"Yes sir, but I think it is worth a try. I owe it to Lucas, and I owe it to you, sir, to try to make this right."

Director Triana continued to stare at his trees. Holstein waited silently. His mouth was dry, but his hands were damp with anxiety.

Without looking at Holstein, Triana said, "Okay, Holstein. I will give you one week."

"Sir. Thank you, sir. I won't let you down."

Triana looked at him and said, "If you do, don't come back. Now get out of here before I change my mind."

Holstein saluted and quickly left the office. Cecelia wouldn't look at him as he passed by her desk.

***

Jake found Frank sitting alone in the bar, nursing a Guinness. He slid his bulk into the booth, bumping the table with his knee. Frank's beer sloshed around in his glass, and a little of the dark brown nectar spilled onto the table.

Looking down at the small puddle, Frank said, "Now that's a shame. You owe me another one."

"Whatever," Jake answered. "I've got good news and bad news."

"What's the good news?"

"The good news is that I'm not fired and you still have a job."

Tilting his head slightly, Frank asked, "So, what's the bad news?"

"I'm not buying you another beer. We leave at 0400."

"Leave? We just got back. Where are we going?"

"We are going to find Vega. And maybe, find Lucas."

Frank smiled. "Sweet." He finished his beer in one long pull, and held up the empty mug. "But you're paying for this one."

***

The small battleship-gray jet touched down smoothly on the hot tarmac of the Posadas airstrip. It taxied to a deserted section and powered down. The two passengers had to wait for a rolling staircase to meet up with the exit hatch.

Stepping out first, Jake tested the stability of the metal steps before putting his full weight onto the staircase. Frank passed Jake's backpack through the hatch. A moment later, he passed two long metal cases through the opening. Climbing down the stairs, Frank said, "Well, the weather hasn't changed. A wet sauna, complete with the delicious odor of rotting fish."

Jake ignored him, while scanning 360 degrees, checking for potential threats.

Frank complained, "Hey. Where is our welcoming committee?"

"Be happy, Frank. No one is shooting at us."

A few minutes later, two men in federal uniforms in a Jeep pulled up. They each carried AK-47s, the rifle of choice for third-world soldiers everywhere. Jake handed a thick envelope to the man in the passenger seat. The driver kept his rifle pointed upward, his finger on the trigger.

The man opened the envelope and peeked inside. Slipping the envelope inside his shirt, he gestured to the two Americans to get into the back of the jeep.

The Federales drove the men outside the airport, to a small nearby warehouse. After exiting the Jeep and unloading their gear, the two Americans waited until the passenger handed a key to Jake. The Jeep took off in a hurry.

Frank said, "Friendly fellas. How much did you tip them?"

Jake replied, "A couple of grand." Reaching into his breast pocket, he pulled out a wad of twenties and held it up. "Minus my finder's fee."

"Holy crap. I'm glad he didn't count it first," Frank said.

"No worries. It's expected down here." He slipped the money back into his pocket, and pointed to the warehouse. "Let's check it out."

The building was a white-washed concrete block structure. It had a low pitched metal roof with generous overhangs. Behind the building, it was a short walk to the Parana River. To the north, they could make out the bridge leading into Paraguay. The front of the building consisted of a small window with iron bars, a metal entrance door, and a battered sectional steel garage door.

Jake inserted the key into the entrance door and pushed it inwards. Reaching around the corner, he found the light switch and flipped it on. A hanging fluorescent light bar buzzed and flickered, finally lighting up the small front office. The room contained a small folding table and several metal chairs. Behind the table, another metal door led to sleeping quarters, a small kitchenette, and a bathroom. A second metal door on the right led to the garage.

Frank closed the entrance door and looked around. "Nice. It reminds me of your apartment."

Jake shook his head. He was irritable and stiff from the long flight, and in no mood for Frank's biting humor. He flipped up a set of switches on the wall, and the lights in the garage turned on instantly.

Moving into the garage, Frank smiled when he saw a Jeep and a modified olive drab 4WD diesel Suburban. The windows on the SUV were heavily tinted. A couple of long wooden crates lined the wall to his left.

"Oh yeah. Now we're talking." Frank said as he walked around to the driver's side of the Suburban and popped the hood. Looking at the engine he said, "Uncle Sam got us a turbo."

Jake walked back to the sleeping quarters, leaving Frank to enjoy his new toys. Rolling up his sleeves, Frank spent the next thirty minutes checking out the engines and drive trains. He talked to the engines as if they were old friends. He didn't even notice Jake had left him alone.

Closing the hood on the Suburban when he was finished, Frank smiled and patted the fender. Leaving the garage, he turned out the lights. He noticed a faint light coming from the sleeping quarters. He could hear Jake snoring, even through the metal door. Unzipping a small compartment in his pack, he felt around until he found a set of earplugs. It was going to be a long, restless night.

Frank woke up first and crawled out of the bed. He dressed quietly, resisting the urge to throw a boot at Jake. Shuffling down the hall, he turned on the lights in the small kitchen. He was surprised to see a full-sized refrigerator. Exploring the cabinets and drawers, he found that the place was fully stocked. On top of the fridge was a loaf of multigrain bread.

Opening the fridge, he stood back and let out a low whistle. There were two 18 packs of large eggs, packages of bacon, breakfast sausage, cartons of milk and orange juice, real butter, jars of orange marmalade and pomegranate jam. The best part was a case of beer and a 12 pack of Guinness. *Thank you, Cecelia.*

Frank got to work making breakfast. When it was almost ready, he went back to the sleeping quarters. Jake was still snoring. *You had your chance, buddy.* Frank picked up one of Jake's boots and threw it at him from across the room before running back to the kitchen. He heard a load roar, and then calmly dropped bread slices into the toaster.

As Frank was flipping the eggs over, Jake stumbled into the kitchen, looking like he'd been out all night drinking. He was holding one of his boots in his hand. "You know anything about this?"

Frank turned around, and with his best innocent look, said, "Hi Jake. You're up. Want some breakfast?"

Jake looked confused, and examined his boot. Shaking his head, as if to clear his mind, he croaked, "Breakfast? Yeah, sure." He sat down with a groan at the small kitchen table.

Frank poured him a cup of coffee. Jake hung his head over the cup inhaling the steam. He downed half of a cup before asking, "Where'd the food come from?"

Frank lied, "Oh, I got up early and went shopping for supplies. I assume you want four eggs?"

They ate their breakfast in silence. When they were finished, Frank said, "I cooked. You clean up." He left the kitchen before Jake could respond.

They each took showers before sitting down to make their plans. They decided to wait until late afternoon to begin their search.

***

They left the warehouse in separate vehicles. Frank drove the SUV. They were looking for Vega, and had a least a dozen places to check. The plan was, whoever spotted him first, would call the other one, then meet up before confronting him. They both dressed in civilian clothes to try to not draw attention to themselves. Under their shirts, they concealed one pistol each, with spare magazines in their pockets.

Jake drove to the north end of town, while Frank started at the south end. Posadas had over 350,000 residents, so they were not too hopeful about finding one man. Asking around, Jake learned that military guys liked to hang out in a section of the city that had plentiful bars. He decided to start there.

Two hours later, it was getting dark outside. He had two more bars to investigate before moving further south. The next one on his list was near the river, the Posadena bar. The music was too loud even before he pushed through the doors. There was a live band playing funkadelic music. Jake preferred country music to this noise.

He spotted a lot of men in military fatigues at the bar and a lot of women with too much makeup and too few clothes. Ordering a beer from the harried bartender, he told her he was looking for his friend, Captain Vega. Her brown eyes darted around the bar before shaking her head 'no'.

Walking to the back of the room, he stood next to the hallway to the bathrooms. Searching the faces of the men on the dance floor, he saw no one who looked like Vega. Setting his empty beer bottle on the bar, he walked back to the bathroom. It was surprisingly empty. There were a dozen urinals against the wall and half as many stalls. Choosing a urinal at the end, he started to relieve himself.

He never heard the man come in from behind him. A garrote looped over his head, and Jake barely got his left hand up in time to keep it from closing around his throat. He sensed the raw strength of his assailant as the wire bit into his left hand. He instinctively stomped on the top of the man's foot, trying to break his hold.

Blood ran down his wrist as he threw himself back, driving his attacker against a metal stall. Throwing his head back, he connected with the man's nose and heard a crunch, as the cartilage broke. The man pushed off from the stall, driving Jake forward toward the urinals. Reaching out with his free hand, Jake stopped his forward momentum.

He groped along the edge of the urinals for anything
he could use as a weapon. His fingers found the neck
of a beer bottle, and he swung it back to where his
attacker's head would be. It connected with a
satisfying thunk, and he swung it again, this time
feeling it break against the man's skull.

Ignoring the pain from the garrote, he stabbed behind
his head with the jagged edge of the broken bottle,
again and again. Jake heard a pained roar, as a warm
gush sprayed against his neck. The grip on the wire
loosened, and Jake swung around, bringing his knee
up in a fluid motion as he flung the garrote away. He
felt his knee connect with the soft flesh of his
attacker's groin, and caught a brief impression of a
hardened, dark skinned face, with blood streaming
from the man's lacerated cheek and right eye.

The attacker swung at him with a fist, but Jake
ducked to the right, and the punch went wide. He
slashed at him with the bottle again, kicking him in
the abdomen with all his might. The attacker's legs
buckled, and he stumbled, hitting his brutalized head
against a urinal as he dropped to one knee.

Stunned, the man reached into his pocket and
extracted a switchblade. The blade snapped open as
he lunged forward. Jake dodged the knife and kicked
him again, this time in the knee. The man crashed
against the urinals again. Without hesitation, Jake
finished him with a roundhouse kick to his head, and
his attacker dropped to the floor unconscious.

Spinning around, Jake scanned the bathroom for any other assailants. The room was still empty.

Grabbing the unconscious man by his shoulders, Jake pulled him into a stall and sat him down on the commode. Grabbing a handful of toilet paper, he jammed it into the door of the stall to keep it shut. The floor of the bathroom was covered in pools of blood. Jake's hand was bleeding badly, but he could move his fingers and make a fist, so no tendons were severed. Sticking his hand under a faucet, he ran the water over his hand and pulled a fistful of paper towels to wrap around his wound.

Looking in the mirror, he saw he had blood running down his neck and the back of his shirt, but knew it wasn't his. Using some wet paper towels, he cleaned up as best he could. He took off his shirt, thankful that his black undershirt would hide the wet blood.

The grip of his pistol was now visible, so he pulled his undershirt up and over the holster. He stuffed his bloody shirt in the trash bin before exiting the bathroom, just as a couple of young men pushed by him to get inside.

Jake headed straight for the door, scanning the room for any other attackers. Once on the sidewalk, he walked quickly towards the Jeep parked three blocks away. Every several yards, he checked behind him to make sure he wasn't being followed.

Waves of inebriated locals staggered tipsily down the sidewalks, a few of them bumping into him as they passed. His hand throbbed with pain as he considered his options. He ducked into a clothing store and purchased a new short-sleeved shirt in muted dark colors. He put it on without buttoning the front.

Leaving the store, he spotted suspicious movement on the sidewalk, one hundred feet ahead of him. Two men with shaved heads were wearing windbreakers, despite the high temperatures. .

The doorway to another bar, El Guapo, was just a few more yards on his right. Music and laughter poured out in waves from within, and it sounded packed, which could work in his favor. He slipped past a group of drinkers standing around tables on the front patio, and pushed his way inside. Ignoring the protests of the party goers, he muscled his way through to the back patio.

Jake leaped over the low retaining wall into the rearing parking lot. Ducking low between the cars, he made his way to the left down a narrow alleyway. A chunk of mortar tore off the brick wall next to him, and he heard the distinctive sound of a ricochet. He shifted into to a flat-out run to put distance between himself and the shooter. Another shot missed by a wider margin. He glanced over his shoulder. The gunman was firing a silenced pistol from behind the bar he just left.

Jake raced to the end of the long alleyway rather than shooting back. His pistol did not have a suppressor, and he didn't want to risk drawing attention to himself. That plan lasted only a few seconds though. Turning the corner, his Jeep was within sight. He thought he was home free until he saw another man in a windbreaker, thirty yards away, running right toward him, a pistol in his hand. *Damn. They must have radios.* Drawing his pistol, Jake made a sharp right turn before raising his sights.

The gunman hesitated for a split second, and Jake fired twice. One of the rounds went wild, but the second connected, and the gunman went down, shooting even as he dropped. Jake felt a tug at the bottom of his new shirt, and he saw hole in the loose material. The bullet had missed him by no more than an inch, which was good enough, but still too close. Jake heard another round zip past his head as the shooter kept trying to hit him. Moving in a zigzag pattern, Jake got a few yards closer to man, aimed carefully, and fired. The man jerked and fell, his weapon skittering across the sidewalk. He then he lay motionless.

People on the sidewalk were now screaming and running in every direction. Glancing over his shoulder, Jake saw that the alleyway was still empty. Crouching low, he ran to his Jeep and jumped in, setting his pistol down on the passenger seat. He turned the key and slammed the shifter into first gear. He pulled out of the parking lot as quickly as he could go without drawing any more attention to himself.

Once on the road, he made several right turns to make sure he wasn't being followed. After he drove for five minutes, he pulled off into a parking lot and called Frank, who picked up on the second ring.

"Frank. Shots fired. I'm okay, but someone is after me. Abort. Repeat, abort."

"Copy that." Frank replied. "I drew a blank anyway. Meet you back at the ranch?"

"Affirmative," Jake said. "Watch for tails," and then he hung up.

***

A few blocks from the warehouse, Frank spotted Jake's Jeep a few cars ahead. They pulled into the entrance as Jake pushed the button on the remote. The garage door creaked its way upward, as the lights came on automatically. Swinging the Jeep around, he backed into the garage. Frank backed up in front of him and killed the engine as Jake closed the garage door.

Frank jumped out of the SUV as Jake was exiting the Jeep. Seeing the bloody paper towels around Jake's left hand, Frank said, "Nice shirt. What happened?"

"I cut myself shaving." Jake holstered his pistol, on his way toward the bathroom. As he entered the front office, the barrel of a rifle pushed against his forehead, backing him up into the garage. Frank started reaching for his pistol, stopping when two more men with rifles, pointed at his face, emerged from the office. Three more men followed behind, pistols drawn and pointed at Jake and Frank, who were now both raising their hands. One of the men relieved them of their pistols.

A moment later, Vega strode into the garage. With his hands on his hips, he glared at his two captives. "Frank and Jake. Frick and Frack, welcome back."

Jake smiled brightly and said, "Vega. Thank God you're alive. We thought they killed you." He started to lower his hands, but the rifle pressed hard against his head. He raised his hands back up. "We looked for you, but couldn't find you. I thought the attackers captured you."

Vega looked at him curiously. "Attackers?"

Jake said, "Yeah, the attackers, the rival cartel. Maybe members of the group we ambushed. They killed your soldiers and killed ten of my men. Lucas was badly wounded, and I guess they got him too. Frank and I barely got out of there alive."

Vega stared into his eyes. Jake could see that he was thinking hard.

Jake continued, "We came back to try to find you and Lucas. We've been all over town trying to get intel.

The cartel is still after us. Look." Jake pointed to his bloody hand. "They ambushed me in a bar."

Vega turned to Frank, who was nodding and trying to look innocent. Frank had practiced that face many times and was good at it.

Vega crossed his arms across his chest and stared into Frank's eyes for a few moments. Frank thought he looked like a reptile, but did not change his innocent expression. Vega turned and walked over to Jake, looking up into his eyes. "You tried to find me?"

"Yeah, buddy. What happened to you? Have you seen Lucas? Is he still alive?"

Vegas thought for a moment and said. "I was out in the jungle, taking a piss, when the attack started. I did not have my rifle, so I could not help. I thought everyone was killed, so I went deeper into the jungle and waited." Vega looked down. Jake could tell that he was lying.

"After an hour, I heard a truck start up and drive away. I waited another thirty minutes before making my way back to the camp. All of the vehicles were disabled. It took me almost a day to walk back to Posadas."

Jake said, "That was us in the truck. Lucas was badly injured. If I had known you were alive, I would have waited for you. Sorry buddy. Hey, no hard feelings, right?"

Vegas looked back and forth at the two men. Finally, he waved his arms at his men, telling them to lower their weapons. Jake slowly walked over to Vega, reaching out his arms to give him a hug. Vega's eyes widened slightly, and he shook his head, signaling, 'Not in front of my men.'

Jake stopped as requested, and reached out his hand to shake, and Vega accepted the gesture. Frank let out a sigh and said, "Jesus, Vega. I'd hate to get on your bad side."

Once again, Jake asked, "Have you seen Lucas?"

Vega shook his head, "No."

"We've got to find him. He's been out there for weeks if he's still alive. That is unless the other cartel got him. Who were those guys?"

Vega shook his head again. "I'm not sure. There is a violent cartel from down south, around Mendoza. They have been shipping drugs into Paraguay. Maybe it's them."

Jake said, "I've got to find out what happened to Lucas. Can you help?"

Vega nodded, "I can ask around."

Jake said, "Frank and I are going back up to the camp, first thing in the morning. Do you want to come along?"

Vega replied, "No, I have much work to do here. But I will send a couple of my men over in the morning. They know the jungle well, and perhaps they will be of some assistance." He turned to leave, signaling his men to follow him. Vega and his men left, going through the front door.

Jake called out to him, "Thanks, buddy."

Without turning around, Vegas raised an arm in acknowledgment.

Frank said, "Nice one, Jake. Do you think he believed you?

"Probably not. But he may think that he still has a use for us, and of course, our big American money and weapons."

"Mutual mistrust. Well I'm not turning my back on him. Hey, let's take a look at your hand."

.

Chapter 11

The Arcum Deus

Lucas closed the book, glancing at his name on the cover. He felt like his world had been turned upside down. He began wondering who his father really was. His father never told him that he had been to Argentina. *What had he been doing down here?*

Watching Lucas carefully, with a concerned look on his face, Hanz said, "I know it is a lot to take in. You have had no preparation, no warning. But then, neither did I. I was a young man, about your age, when the Brujos took me in."

Hanz walked over to the map of South America. Pointing to the north east section of Argentina, he said, "Look here. We are here," pointing slightly northwest of Posadas. "The nearest Arcum Deus, or 'door of the gods,' is here, outside Salta, at the foot of the Andes. It is a five-hour flight to Salta. We must then travel by car for four hours to get to Cerro Tuzgle, an extinct volcano."

Hanz continued. "I do not think you will believe me until you see for yourself. Once you see what I have to show you, then you will have enough information to make up your mind. There is only one thing I must ask of you."

Lucas replied, "What is that?'

"You must swear that you will not tell anyone what you see there. This has been a blood secret of the Brujos for centuries. It is even more imperative now, that this must be kept a secret. If the Brujos Negro find out, it will be a disaster for everyone."

"If I say no, not no to the secret, but if I decide against going with you to this volcano, will you take me back to Posadas to find my companions?"

Hanz was crestfallen. He was so sure Lucas would want to join him, and he was not expecting him to turn his back on this opportunity.

"If that is what you wish, we will not hold you here against your will. We will take you to find your friends."

"Thank you. That is the answer I was looking for." Lucas stood up. "I would like to sleep on it, and I will give you an answer in the morning."   He was still holding on to the book. "May I take this back to my room?"

"Of course. You may keep it as long as you wish. Please, before you go, may I change your bandages?"

Lucas instinctively placed his hand over his wounds. They were still tender, and now he noticed that they were itching. He replied, "Yes, please."

Hanz motioned him over to the desk as he raised a small basket from the floor. "Please, lift up your robe."

Lucas was not comfortable wearing something akin to a dress. Now Hanz was asking him to lift it up. Overcoming his embarrassment, he did as he was asked. Hanz carefully removed the bandages and poured a brown liquid onto a clean cloth. He cleaned the wounds and Lucas felt a tingling sensation as the liquid touched his skin. In seconds, the wounds felt numb. Lucas frowned. Something about Hanz made Lucas want to trust him. He had been nothing but gentle and gracious. Hanz selected another bottle from the basket and poured a thick greenish substance onto two fresh gauze pads. Carefully placing the pads over the wounds, he secured them with some tape. "Soon you will be as good as new."

"Thank you, and thank you for the dinner. I am sorry, but I must excuse myself. I am exhausted."

Lucas left the study and walked outside. There was enough moonlight to illuminate his way back to his room. Switching on the light, he closed the door to his room. He set the book down on the small table. Sitting on his bed, he realized that he was more exhausted than he realized. He switched off the light. Lying down, he closed his eyes and was asleep within seconds.

***

Chapter 11 The Arca Deus

Lucas awakened with a start, and sat up. His heart was pounding, and his skin was covered with a film of sweat. He thought he must have had a nightmare, but could not remember any of it. Swinging his legs to the floor, he walked to the door and stepped outside. There were no lights coming from the stone house. The air was still, hot, and wet. The moon had set, and the star fields were brilliant. Looking up to the heavens, Lucas felt Orion beckoning to him. He waited, but the hunter provided no answers. His eyes drifted to Scorpio and he shivered involuntarily.

Back in his bed, he perused the book for an hour. There were photos of his childhood he had never seen before. Old memories came flooding into his brain. Some of the photos made him laugh, and some triggered feelings of sadness and loss. Somehow, there were photos of him in recent years. A few had to be classified. He wondered how Hanz had obtained them. His eyes became heavy and he reviewed his recent life before falling asleep.

***

Momentarily disoriented, Lucas listened carefully before opening his eyes. Confirming that he was alone in the room, he rolled out of bed. His wounds still hurt, but not nearly as much as yesterday. Pouring water into a glass, he drank thirstily, before slipping on the brown robe. Walking silently to the door, he opened it a crack. It was still dark, but the eastern sky was showing signs of the coming morning. Seeing no one outside, he walked to the edge of the jungle and relieved himself.

Finding a flat open area, he began moving through his morning exercise routine. His mind worked rapidly, as he sorted through his options, and the potential consequences of the decisions he had to make. One path had him trying to contact Jake or the Director. A branch of that path had him hunting down Vega. Another branch had him finding a way to return to the agency to get medical help. Another path had him going with Hanz to that volcano, which might prove that Hanz was either sane or delusional. If Hanz was delusional, then he could go back and take the first path. If Hanz turned out to be sane, Lucas was not sure where that new path would lead him. He did not have enough information, and there was only one way to get it.

Sometimes, Lucas cursed his insatiable curiosity. It had gotten him in trouble before, but it often brought unexpected rewards. Looking back, he had survived the troubles, and he had benefited from the rewards. As much as he prided himself on his ability to use logic, he realized that his curiosity often overrode his reason.

Finishing his exercises with the yoga routine, surya namaskar, the salute to the sun, he noticed Hanz watching him from the porch of the stone building. The old man waved him over. *I guess I'm going with curiosity.*

Lucas waited for the blessings to end this time, before digging into the meal. He recognized the chicken eggs, but the offerings also included some yellow melons and an unrecognizable grilled meat. Lucas asked about it and was told it was capybara, which didn't help.

After the meal was over, one of the men handed Lucas a basket. It contained a pair of dark tan cargo pants, a white t-shirt, wool socks, and a long sleeved beige cotton shirt. Another man handed him his tactical boots and his belt, both of which had been cleaned. Noticing the puzzled look on Lucas' face, Hanz said, "Your fatigues were ruined, but we saved your boots and belt. We brought you more civilian-looking clothes so that you can blend in during our travels."

Giving Hanz a hard look, Lucas said, "I did not say I was going."

Hanz replied, "You did not say you weren't. I took that as a yes."

Nodding, Lucas asked, "So when do we leave?"

"Now would be good, if we want to catch our flight. You can get dressed in my study."

Lucas dressed quickly, surprised that the clothes fit him. There was something missing and it made him feel vulnerable. He had no firearm, and there were still enemies out there. They would be driving to

Posadas, and then flying, and then driving again into a wilderness area, leaving them open to attack. He expressed his concern to Hanz.

Hanz listened, and then replied, "Do not worry. We will be protected along the way. We must go now."

Lucas followed Hanz and two of his men outside. They were all dressed in civilian clothing. Another man was standing next to the driver's side of a black, mud encrusted Suburban, with heavily tinted windows.

"Where did that come from?" Lucas asked.

Hanz flashed him a sly smile and replied, "I know a guy."

"Somehow, that doesn't surprise me."

Lucas sat in the back, with Hanz and one of the men, the other two men got into the front, and the driver started the engine. Lucas noted that the vehicle was four wheel drive, and sounded like a diesel. He also noted the shotgun and two rifles in the front seat. They arrived at the airport in less than an hour. As soon as the men got out of the Suburban, the driver took off. Hanz and two of the men escorted Lucas through the terminal and onto the waiting commercial aircraft.

The flight was uneventful, and Lucas marveled at the beautiful countryside below. This part of Argentina was sparsely populated, with just a few farms and ranches scattered across huge verdant valleys. As they approach Salta, Lucas could see the towering Andes Mountains in the distance.

The upper slopes were covered in snow and ice, and he could make out several large muddy rivers flowing down into the valley below. There were a number of small lakes surrounding the city.

The plane banked for final approach into Salta. Hanz pointed to the hills west of the city and said, "Your American film, Tarus Bulba, with Yul Brynner and Tony Curtis, was filmed in those hills." Lucas gave him a quizzical look. Hanz, lifted his nose and said, "I have not been totally isolated from your culture."

The plane landed with only a slight bounce, and taxied to the terminal, which was much larger than Lucas expected. Hanz' men waited for the baggage, while Hanz walked Lucas outside. Lucas looked around nervously, alert for potential threats. The air was cool and dry, a welcome contrast to the steamy jungle they left behind. Lucas was not surprised to see a black four-wheel drive Suburban pull up to the curb in front of them. A second black Suburban pulled in behind the first. Two large men got out of it and scanned the surrounding area. They were wearing dark sunglasses, and their jackets had tell-tale bulges over their hips.

Hanz' men arrived from baggage claim, bringing eight large duffle bags on a cart. They loaded the bags into the back of the Suburbans and climbed inside. One of the men from the second Suburban handed Hanz a large covered basket. They wasted little time before the two vehicles left the airport. Soon they were driving on highway 51, first heading west southwest. The road wound around through some small towns, and then they headed northwest into the mountains.

Hanz opened the basket and began handing out sandwiches and bottles of water. After an hour, they stopped in the small town of Campo Quijano for a restroom break. As they were getting back into the vehicle, one of the men handed a towel-wrapped heavy package to Lucas. Lucas opened the towel and found his pistol, holster, and several loaded magazines. Someone had taken the time to give it a thorough cleaning. As Lucas brightened, the man smiled. Looking around, to make sure no one else was watching, Lucas performed a chamber check and a magazine check. The pistol was ready for action. He strapped the holster to his belt. His sense of vulnerability finally left him.

In another hour, they turned north on highway 40. Soon, they approached what Hanz called the Viaducto de la Povorilla, and an incredible bridge of the Tren a las Nubes, or Train to the Clouds came into view. It spanned a gorge over 200 feet below. Hanz said, "A long time ago, this was Inca territory." Lucas wanted to take photos, but he had no camera. He noticed that it was getting harder to breathe at this altitude. He started taking deeper and more frequent breaths.

A short time later, the driver pulled to the side of the road. To the right was the large snow capped volcano, Cerro Tuzgle. On one side of the volcano, there were black latitic lava flows.

Hanz stated, "The summit is one foot short of 18,000 feet above sea level." He automatically translated meters into feet. "I do not know why God did not add a little more dirt to make it even. We will not be going that high. Already, we are at about 13,000 feet. It is time to break out our parkas."

The man in the shotgun seat exited the vehicle, and walked to the back of the Suburban, opening the rear doors. He pulled four parkas out of one of the duffle bags. He slipped into one of the parkas and handed three more to Hanz. Lucas felt the cold air enter the vehicle, and began to shiver. He quickly put on his parka and zipped it up. It had a built-in hood, with a fur edging. The man in the back unzipped another duffle bag and pulled out four backpacks. He handed three of them to Hanz, one at a time.

Looking inside the pack, Lucas found containers of water, bags of dried fruit and nuts, flashlights, extra batteries, packs of dried meat, emergency blankets, goggles, and a first aid kit. The three men climbed out of the vehicle. The six men in the second Suburban had already geared up and walked over. They were each carrying M16 rifles strapped to their bodies. Two of the men had large packs on their backs.

Hanz whispered something to the man at the rear of the Suburban. Lucas thought the man turned red before reaching into the back deck. He unzipped another duffle bag and produced 4 more M16s. He passed the rifles around. He then found a dozen loaded magazines and handed them out as well. He then strapped a large pack onto his back.

Lucas turned to Hanz, "Are we expecting trouble?"

Hanz replied, "I was never a Boy Scout, but I like their motto, 'be prepared'. I recommend we each drink a liter of water now."

They all drank water and left the empty bottles in the vehicles. Two of the men stayed behind and soon drove off.

As they were pulling away, Lucas asked, "Where are they going?

Hanz replied, "They are taking the vehicles down the road and will pull off and hide them behind some outcroppings. We do not want to show anyone else where we are going." Hanz did a 360 degree scan to make sure no one was watching, put on his goggles, and then turned and headed toward the lava flows.

He stopped every thirty minutes to rest and let everyone catch their breath. The sun was starting to drop behind the Andes. After hiking for two hours, Hanz stopped and said, "When we left Posadas this morning, we were barely 500 feet above sea level.

We acclimated at little on the airplane, which was pressurized to 8,000 feet, but our bodies have not adjusted to this altitude. We must stop here and spend the night.

The men with the large duffle bags unzipped them and produced five two-man tents and a pile of sleeping bags. They had the tents set up in ten minutes. Just as they were finishing, the two drivers came hiking over a hill and joined them. They too were carrying large duffle bags. Unzipping them, they pulled out petrol cooking stoves, pots, and bags of food. Within minutes, they had the stoves fired up and set up the two large pots on aluminum stands. They poured some of the food in each pot and added water.

Several of the men left and shortly returned with armloads of wood for a fire. They had it blazing in fifteen minutes. The fire was small, so they sat close to it. Lucas was happy for the warmth, as the temperature was dropping drastically after the sun set. As the men gathered around the fire, the cooks dished out food into aluminum bowls.

Once everyone was served, Hanz said the blessing in Spanish and English. Lucas said, "You do know I speak Spanish fluently."

"Yes, but I think God does not mind two blessings."

Lucas noticed that the men took their time eating again. He tried to slow down himself, and noticed how much better the food tasted when he closed his eyes and focused on the textures and taste of the individual components of their meal. When he was finished, Lucas looked up into the star fields, seeing them more clearly than he could ever remember, knowing it was because of the thin mountain air.

Hanz noticed him and asked, "Do you have a favorite?"

Without looking at Hanz, Lucas replied, "Yes. I always try to find Orion."

Hanz said, "Oh yes, Orion, the hunter. I think that is a good choice for you, Lucas."

Lucas nodded. "And which one do you always look for?'

Hanz laughed, and replied, "I always try to find Pyxis Nautica, the mariners' compass." He pointed, "You see those three bright stars in a line? They are Alpha, Beta, and Gamma Pyxidis. When I feel lost, I try to find my stars. Somehow, it makes me think, and I become centered again."

"Well, I feel centered as well, when I see Orion. But lately, I find I can no longer just see Orion. My eyes always drift to the constellation Scorpio. Scorpio was Orion's enemy, and eventually killed him."

"So the hunter is also the hunted?"

Lucas nodded. "That is why I know I must be ever vigilant. At any time, when I am focused on my prey, the scorpion may strike."

Hanz replied, "Maybe that is why my eyes always drift to the constellation Phoenix." He pointed to the constellation. "Phoenix, the firebird; the one that keeps being reborn." The men were quiet for a while. Then Hanz spoke. "You are welcome to share my Phoenix, Lucas Forge. Whenever you fear you are beaten, you may rise again like the Phoenix."

Lucas stared at the Phoenix constellation, and felt a deep sense of comfort.

Hanz said, "I must rest now. We will be starting again early in the morning." He stood up and went to his tent.

Lucas stared at the constellations for another hour. The fire had burned down to coals, and most of the other men had retreated to their tents. He saw two of the men standing guard. Walking over to one of the men he said, "Let me know when it is my turn to stand watch." The man looked at him a moment, and then nodded.

***

Lucas woke up before dawn as usual. No one had awakened him for guard duty. He dressed quietly so as not to wake Hanz. Leaving the tent, he found a jug of water and drank at least a liter. Two different men, the two who were the drivers, were now standing watch, and the fire was burning hot. One of them had put a coffee pot near the fire, and Lucas could smell the inviting aroma. Lucas grabbed his rifle. Walking behind a large bush, he relieved himself. He found a small flat spot and performed his morning exercises. When he was finished, he walked back to the fire and poured himself a cup of steaming coffee. Moving over to one of the men, he tapped him on the shoulder and waved him over to the fire. The man nodded, and left Lucas to stand post.

The sun began to paint the sky with blues and pinks. The men in the camp began to rise and stumble around the fire, pouring cups of coffee. Lucas watched as the men found their own places to sit, but they sat silently, without interacting with each other. One of the cooks made himself busy preparing their breakfast, and soon, the aroma of bacon and eggs floated through camp.

After the blessing, the men ate their breakfast in silence. The camp was taken down and they were on their way to the lava field. Hanz led the way and set the pace. Lucas tried to engage several men in conversation without much success. The men were friendly, but contributed very little to any topics Lucas broached. He resigned himself to walking in silence. Shortly, he was thankful, as the trail steepened, and he had to breathe heavily and rapidly to keep oxygen flowing to his brain.

When the sun was directly overhead, Hanz made a sharp turn to the left. There was no visible trail, but he seemed to know where he was going. The men behind him spread out to avoid creating an obvious track. The angle of the slope increased dramatically, and Lucas found himself grabbing onto rocks and boulders to make his way upward. His pace slowed and he began counting his breaths between steps. Hanz moved steadily upward, seemingly immune to the altitude. Soon he was far ahead of the group and disappeared over a steep rise.

The men were passing Lucas on both sides, and soon he was at the end of the procession. All of the men disappeared over a large pile of black lava rocks. Lucas wanted to cry out, 'wait up,' but did not want to appear weak. He was almost hyperventilating now, trying to force scarce molecules of oxygen into his lungs. He had to stop every ten paces to catch his breath. Finally, he crested the pile of lava and looked down at the men, who were all sitting down in a rough circle. Hanz was standing and drinking water out of a bottle. Lucas worked his way down to the men and sat down, struggling to not fall over with exhaustion, and pretended that he was not out of breath.

Hanz pointed to a large flat shiny rock in the side of a large tubular flow of hardened lava. "This is it, Lucas. This is the entrance to the Arcum Deus."

Hanz and one of the men climbed up to the shiny rock. Lucas now saw that the rock was circular, and it seemed so smooth and shiny that it roughly reflected the image of Hanz as he stood in front of it. Hanz and the man grabbed at the left side of the shiny circle and pulled to the right. The rock rolled along a track, revealing a black opening. Hanz slipped inside and disappeared. The rest of the men followed, while the one man held the doorway open.

Lucas was dumfounded. He found himself moving forward without thinking. Ducking his head, he entered the black hole. The men had turned on their flashlights which illuminated a tunnel that dropped off steeply. The man holding the rock stepped inside, and the rock rolled back into place. Hanz led the men downward for twenty paces and then turned left at the entrance to a lava tube that ran left to right. The right side of the tube sloped downward. The route that Hanz took sloped upward.

Hanz moved forward faster and faster. Lucas struggled to keep up with the men in front of him. After trudging upward through the tube for fifteen minutes, he saw the men slow down and then stop. Lucas walked forward past them to reach Hanz. The old man stood at the threshold of an opening into a shiny room. He was taking off his pack and parka. When Lucas reached him, Hanz pointed his flashlight inside.

"Welcome, Lucas, to the Arcum Deus."

Pointing his flashlight forward and then around in a large arc, Lucas viewed a large room that seemed to be made of a metallic substance. He knew that this room was unnatural. Someone made this. The floor was flat and the walls were rounded. In the center of the room, there stood a tall monolithic structure. It looked like a wall within the chamber. It was flat and gray and stood about eight feet tall and three or four feet wide. The sides and top were covered in various tiles about one foot by one foot square. It reminded Lucas of an ornate door. Taking off his pack and parka and moving forward, Lucas saw that the tiles had odd markings on them that looked like some form of ancient writing.

There was a wide wooden table to the right, and on the surface were various bottles, boxes and unrecognizable objects. Two of the men reached into their packs, removing boxes, and then placing the boxes under the table.

Hanz was smiling, watching Lucas' face. The rest of the men moved into a semi-circle around the tall monolith. They were now wearing brown robes. Hanz nodded to the men and they began singing in an unknown language. The walls of the room started to light up and change colors. The room began vibrating in time with the song. Suddenly, Lucas felt a tugging at his wounds. He dropped to his knees as his whole body started vibrating. The colors began to swirl around the room like a whirlpool.

The men started singing louder and the words were coming faster and faster. Hanz had somehow changed into a white robe. The monolith changed from gray to swirling colors. Lucas was transfixed, mesmerized by the ever changing colors. Hanz looked at his watch, and then walked to the monolith and pressed one of the tiles. Without warning, the colors disappeared and the formerly colorful surface of the monolith now became clear. Lucas could see through it into the other side of the room, At first, he thought the surface had become transparent, but Hanz walked behind the monolith and Lucas could not see him. *What sort of trick is he pulling?*

Staring into the transparency, Lucas suddenly saw an old, tall, dark skinned man in a white robe walk into view on the other side of the monolith. It was not Hanz. Behind the tall man were a dozen men in brown robes, and he could now hear them singing.

The tall man looked at his watch and then moved forward, raising a hand. He did something to the edge of the monolith on his side. He waited a moment, and then stepped through the transparent opening and stood in front of Lucas. The singing stopped and the monolith immediately turned back to an opaque gray. The vibrations stopped. Hanz stepped back from behind the monolith and walked forward toward Lucas. The tall man turned and hugged Hanz. They spoke in whispers for a few moments.

Lucas noticed that the pain from his wounds was gone. He reached down and pushed at his wounds. Lifting up his shirt, and ripping off bandages, he saw no evidence that he had been shot. There were no scars. He felt the room spinning around him and he fell over. Looking up at the rounded ceiling, he passed out.

***

"Wake up, Lucas."

Lucas recognized Hanz' voice and opened his eyes. Hanz was kneeling down beside him, holding his hand. He said gently, "I know it is a lot to take in. But you are strong, and I need you to sit up."

Lucas obeyed without thinking, and sat up. Everyone in the room was still sitting down in a circle around him. Lucas remembered what had happened, and checked his wounds again. He had not been dreaming. He was healed as if nothing had happened to him.

He screamed at Hanz, "What the hell is going on?"

"It is not hell, Lucas. It may be the opposite. What do you think?

"I think this is a dream. Or, you drugged me. This cannot be happening."

"It is not a dream, Lucas. We did not drug you. This is the Arcum Deus." Hanz pulled up his white robe, and pointed to his leg. "This was badly broken when I was your age. Do you see any evidence of a fracture?"

152

Looking down at Hanz' leg, Lucas said, "No. But you could have been lying to me about breaking your leg."

"And you could have been lying to me about being shot?"

Lucas was at a loss for words. Putting his head in his hands, he began to rock back and forth.

"Lucas, this is real. It is just, not the reality that you have known. I cannot explain it to you in terms that you recognize. You must open your mind and accept what you see with your own eyes."

Lucas looked up at Hanz, who was smiling gently. Turning his head, he saw the tall man, who was almost grinning. Lucas said, "What? You think this is funny?'

The man replied in a Spanish accent, "I think it is very funny. I once sat where you are. I had been stabbed repeatedly and was dying. I was brought to a room like this, and I too was healed. This is very funny business, don't you think?"

Lucas looked down in disgust, "No, no, no. This cannot be happening." He slapped himself hard across his face.

Hanz handed him a water bottle. "Drink now and regain your strength. I will let you think for a while."

Hanz stood up and walked to the table. The tall man followed him. They spoke in whispers for a long while.

When Lucas finally looked up, he saw the men around him were slowly rocking back and forth and had their eyes closed. They appeared to be praying. He stood up, feeling stronger and more alert than ever. He looked at the gray monolith and then looked at Hanz talking to the tall man. His curiosity urge was pushing him forward. He walked behind the monolith and saw that nothing was there, but the end of the room.

Moving back over to Hanz, he said, "You know, I thought that you were delusional. Now, I wonder if I am delusional."

Hanz replied, "I understand. It is as if you were blind, and now you see."

Looking at the tall man, Lucas asked, "Where did you come from? I mean, where were you on the other side of that, monolith, that door?"

The man looked at Hanz, who nodded his head. The man replied, "My name is Santiago Delgado. I was in a place called Pinacate, in Mexico."

"Mexico? How could you have come from Mexico?

Santiago smiled. He answered, "I walked through the door of another Arcum Deus."

Shaking his head in disbelief, he asked. "Are you a Brujo?"

"I am a Brujo Blanco. A white sorcerer, in your language."

"Will you teach me how to go through that doorway?"

The man laughed. "Oh, going through the doorway is easy, once you know the song. I have a degree in physics from the university. While there, I learned that all matter vibrates, it is constantly in motion. Everything from the smallest particles, to planets, to the universe; all things are in motion and vibrate. These rooms respond to the sound vibrations in our singing. Our ancestors took many centuries to identify the precise vibrations that active these rooms. The vibrations also resonate with our bodies, aligning the atoms inside of us. The rooms can realign our atoms to fix any irregularities. That is how I was healed, and that is how you and Hanz were healed."

"That is impossible. You are saying that singing some song healed us?" Lucas asked.

"We were healed by the Arcum Deus. You have seen the results, Lucas. You have seen the changes in your own body. I cannot tell you how it works, just that it does. And we can move easily from one Arcum to another." We now know the proper songs, so going through the doorway is just a tool that we can use when needed."

Hanz and the tall man were watching Lucas absorb this information. Lucas looked back and forth at the two men. His face revealed the internal struggle occurring in his mind.

The tall man continued, "To use the door, one must become a Brujo. That is the only way. Becoming a Brujo is much more difficult than walking through these doors. Only Brujos Blanco can use the pathway. One first has to be chosen by two Brujo Superiors, and then, one has to accept the invitation."

Lucas turned to Hanz. "Is that what you are, a Brujo Superior?"

Hanz answered, "Yes, we both are."

"Is that why you brought me here, to offer an invitation?"

Hanz looked at Santiago, and then gazed at Lucas. "Yes, we are inviting you to become a Brujo Blanco."

Lucas stared at the two men for a moment and then looked away. His mind was racing, but every thought was leading him to the same conclusion. It was as if everything he knew was wrong and now he must make a decision based on instinct rather than rational thought. Once again, his curiosity was suppressing his logic and scientific training.

Looking up at the two men, he gave them his answer. "I accept your invitation."

He knew that his life would never be the same.

Chapter 11   The Arca Deus

Chapter 12

The Warehouse; Three weeks earlier

Frank was examining the cut on Jake's hand. "You are going to need stitches, Jake."

"Can't you just wrap some duct tape on it, like you did with Lucas?

At the mention of Lucas' name, Frank felt pangs of guilt. He felt responsible for Lucas' disappearance. "A lot of good it did him."

"Come on, Frank. We are going out tomorrow to look for him. We will find him. I thought Vega had him, but based on his reaction when I asked about Lucas, I believe he genuinely had nothing to do with his disappearance."

"That's the problem. If Vega didn't do it, then who did?" Franks pulled a trauma kit from his backpack. Unzipping the kit, he rifled around the contents. He placed several objects on the table.

He asked, "You don't think Lucas took off on his own, do you?"

Jake shook his head. "No way. He wouldn't just leave us without saying something. Besides, he was hurt too badly. I don't think he was capable of climbing out of the sling and jumping out of the truck. Someone or, more likely, a group of people snatched him."

"But who? And why?"

Jake looked up at the ceiling. "I don't know. Very few people knew he was even down here. Maybe it was some of Vega's men, but I don't think so. It had to be some men from the same cartel we ambushed; the same cartel who then ambushed us. Maybe the same guys who tried to kill me tonight."

While Jake was still looking up, Frank jabbed a needle into Jake's hand and pushed the plunger.

"Hey, holy shit. That hurt." Jake said.

"Don't worry. It will be numb in a minute or so. There is no point in having you screaming while I am trying to sew you up."

"Screaming? I wouldn't scream.'

"Yeah, well, now we'll never know."

Frank poured some disinfectant on the open wound, and watched it bubble and foam. Unwrapping a suture kit, and grabbing the needle with suture thread already loaded, he began to sew the wound closed. It took twelve stitches to finish the job. He poured more disinfectant over the closed wound and wrapped a bandage around his hand. "Can you still move your fingers?"

Jake looked down at his hand, moved each of his fingers, and then lifted up his hand with his middle finger extended upwards.

Frank frowned. "Yeah, well fuck you too. You can sew yourself up next time." Standing up, he said, "I need a Guinness."

Frank went to the cabinet and found two glasses. He set them down on the table. Moving to the refrigerator, he pulled out a Guinness, and a can of the cheaper beer. He handed the cheap can to Jake and sat down. Pulling the tab on the Guinness, Frank listened as the nitrogen ball inside the can hissed. He slowly poured his beer into a glass and studied the frothy head. He watched the bubbles fall on the inside of the glass, and wondered, for the hundredth time, why the bubbles didn't rise.

Lost in their private thoughts, they each had one more beer. After finishing them, Frank stood up and said, "I served, you clean up."

"Hey, I'm wounded."

Frank ignored him, and went to bed, hoping he would fall asleep before the snoring started.

***

Frank got up first, again, and made breakfast before throwing a boot at Jake. Slipping back into the kitchen, he put the steaming plates on the table and sat down. Jake stumbled into the kitchen, holding the boot in his right hand. He glared at Frank, before sitting down to eat.

As soon as they finished, they heard a knock at the door. Both men pulled out their pistols and took aim at the door. A few seconds later, they heard a louder series of knocks. Jake moved to the side of the door, holding his pistol level, while Frank continued to point in.

Jake asked, "Who is it?"

A muffled response came back, "Vega sent us."

Jake reached up, slid the safety latch open, and grasped the door knob with his bandaged hand. Looking at Frank, he waited for him to nod, swinging open the door. He took a step back from the door and raised his sights. He waited for Frank to lower his weapon to the ready, while stepping outside, moving to the left. Jake followed him, out moving to the right. Scanning the area and seeing no threats, only two men in fatigues, standing in front of a Jeep, their arms crossed. Jake holstered his pistol. Frank followed suit, and approached Vega's men. They all shook hands.

One of the men spoke, "We are here to help you find your friend. I know what it is like to lose someone. My brother was killed at the camp." Frank thought he saw the man's eyes become watery. "We have the funeral in two days. I hope your friend is still alive."

"I am sorry for your loss. I will pray for him. What was his name?"

"His name was Rodrigo. He was my younger brother."

"Are you sure you want to go with us? Shouldn't you be with your family?"

"There was only the two of us left. My parents died long ago. My older brother was also killed fighting the cartels. I will not die by their hands, not without killing as many as I can first." He stood a little straighter, as if to emphasize his resolve.

"I would like to help you get them as well. By the way, our friend's name is Lucas." Frank said. "He disappeared somewhere between Vega's camp and the top of the ridge at the end of the jungle. I think we should start at the ridge."

Jake and Frank climbed into the Suburban. Frank naturally took the driver's side. The Jeep pulled out and proceeded to ignore the speed limits the whole way, until hitting the jungle. Pulling off to the side, one of the men got out and walked over to the idling Suburban.

"Is this the spot, when you found him missing?"

Frank nodded. "I should have checked on him earlier, but we were trying to get him to the hospital."

Chapter 12   The Warehouse; 3 Weeks Earlier

The man looked up the road toward the deepening jungle. "Perhaps we should go first. We can follow the road slowly, and look for any traces of what might have happened. You can follow us, or go on ahead, if you think that would help"

Frank replied, "I think we will go on ahead. Here is a radio you can use to communicate with us." Frank handed him one of their spare FM transceivers. "Do you know how to work it?"

The man examined the handset and pushed the talk button. The radio in the Suburban clicked and hissed in response. "Yes, I know this model."

Frank and Jake proceeded to drive up the road, leaving the Jeep far behind. They continued to a sharp turn in the road, where they had to slow down.

Jake said, "Wait. Stop here."

Frank pulled off to the side of the road, as Jake jumped out of the vehicle. Jake began looking at the ground and the surrounded bushes. Frank turned off the engine, and climbed out. Walking slowly, he scanned the rocks and dirt, moving behind Jake.

"Look at this," Jake shouted. He was looking at a thick set of bushes on the left.

Frank reached him as Jake lifted some of the branches of a stand of young guayacan trees. Jake noticed that some of the smaller branches were bent and broken. "Something, or someone, moved through here."

Frank reached down and pulled out a short piece of fiber. It was a dirty white thread. "This is man made."

Jake continued up the road a few paces. He noticed another patch of broken branches on the left. Searching the ground, he found tire tracks, perpendicular to the road. "It looks like a truck turned around here." They memorized the tread marks in the dirt. "It looks like it headed back up the road."

Climbing back into the Suburban, they continued up the road at a slower pace. Jake kept a sharp eye out for any side roads. Finding none after a few miles, Frank began to drive a little faster. It still took them almost two hours to reach the former camp where they were ambushed. The road ended at what was left of the camp. The tents were gone, as were all of the bodies.

Frank said, "Someone cleaned up."

Looking knowingly at each other, Frank made a wide turn and headed back down the road. They met the parked Jeep almost an hour later. The two men from the Jeep were pulling at a thick bunch of bushy plants. Frank stopped the Suburban and they got out. Vega's men pulled the bushes toward the road, revealing a faint two track road.

Chapter 12   The Warehouse; 3 Weeks Earlier

One of Vega's men stated the obvious. "This road was hidden for a reason."

Jake studied the ground and said, "The same truck went this way."

The men returned to their vehicles and began following the two track road, the Jeep leading the way. The jungle was heating up, and their slow speed provided minimal ventilation. Frank turned on the air conditioning. Jake gave him a sideways glance, but said nothing.

"What?" Frank asked. "We never get this kind of luxury on missions. Why not take advantage of it?"

Jake remained silent, concentrating on the hundreds of ways they could be ambushed without ever seeing it coming. His nerves were getting frazzled more and more with every mile they drove. Thick wet branches slapped at the vehicle as if to tell them to go back.

Frank muttered, "I think the jungle wants to take back the road."

Small unidentifiable rodents scurried back and forth across the road in front of them. Each time the furry creatures burst out of the underbrush, Jake tensed up a little more. Adding to his frustration, Frank asked, "What if there is another side road hidden behind some bushes?"

"I'm hoping Vega's men will see it and stop. All we can do is keep going until we find the truck, or get ambushed trying."

A heavy brown blur dropped onto the hood. Jake snapped his rifle into firing position. It was gone in an instant.

"Jesus, Jake. You can't fire that thing in here."

"Why not? If we get attacked, I'm taking out the windshield first."

"Look closely. I forgot to tell you. These windows aren't just tinted, they are bullet proof glass. You shoot in here, and you're going to end up killing me, or yourself."

"This thing's armored?" Jake asked. "No wonder it's riding so heavy. What the hell did the agency think we were getting into down here?

Shaking his head, Frank replied, "Trouble, trouble, and more trouble. We've been lied to, shot at, and you almost got your head cut off. We are following two men with questionable motives. What could go wrong?"

Suddenly Jake said, "Hey. Slow down. It looks like a clearing ahead."

"As I said, trouble and more trouble."

Chapter 12   The Warehouse; 3 Weeks Earlier

The Jeep punched through the jungle into a large open area. At the far side was a large, one story stone building. The Jeep veered to the right and stopped. Vega's men jumped out, rifles pointing toward the structure. Frank pulled forward and turned to the left. A smaller wooden building was directly in front of them. Slamming on the brakes, Frank steered carefully as the heavy truck skidded along the wet grass. Leaping out before the truck stopped fully, Jake went down on one knee, scanning the area with his rifle scope.

Frank climbed out and stayed low, scanning the small building and the surrounding jungle border. He started to move forward, when he felt the muzzle of a rifle dig into the back of his head. A raspy voice said, "Drop your weapon. Now." Frank did as he was told. He felt his pistol being pulled from his holster. The voice continued, "Stand up, slowly."

Frank's mind began to run through the various scenarios whereby he could disarm his assailant without getting his head blown off. Those thoughts evaporated when the man said, "Put your hands behind your back." As he began moving his arms backward, another set of hands grabbed him and fastened zip ties around his wrists. Looking to his right, he saw the same series of events were happening to Jake and to Vega's men.

Their assailants were all wearing brown robes, and looked like monks, rather than the trained professionals that they obviously were. The man with the raspy voice said, "Alright. Everyone walk toward the fortress." Frank took a second look at the stone structure, and realized that it did indeed look like it could be a fortress. Within a minute, they were inside and forced to kneel on the wooden floor.

An old man with a gray beard and long hair came out of a room to the left. Standing in front of the four kneeling men, and speaking in a vaguely German accent he said, "Who are you and why are you here?" Vega's men looked down at the floor. One of the robed men pushed his rifle hard into Jake's head.

Jake answered, "Ok. Ok. Look, we are just trying to find our friend. He was kid...I mean he must have fallen out of the back of our truck a few days ago, and he was badly hurt. We just need to get him to a hospital."

"The old man continued, "Your friend? Who is he, and how was he injured."

Jake looked at Frank for a moment, before the muzzle pushed back into his head. "His name is Lucas. He was shot in a hunting accident. I think he may be dying."

"Why did you come here?"

Jake answered, "We have been going up and down the road where we lost him. We stumbled upon your road and thought maybe he wandered off down here. Please, have you seen him?"

The old man ignored his question. "If this was a hunting accident, why are you armed with assault rifles and pistols?"

Frank decided to help out, "We were told that there were drug runners in the jungle, and we had to be careful. They also said there were wild pigs, so we had back up pistols, in case we needed to protect ourselves."

The old man turned around and had a whispered conversation with one of the other men. Looking over his shoulder at Jake, he grabbed the other man's elbow and they moved into a room off to the right. They continued their conversation, and it began to get heated. Jake looked over at Frank. His expression signaled that he was thinking about trying to escape. Frank shook his head no.

The old man returned and glared at each of the men, one by one. "My associate thinks we should kill you and bury your bodies in the jungle." Again, he stared at each of the four men.

"I, however, think that you are just foolish men. I assure you, we have not seen your friend. We are very protective of our privacy here, and we have to be careful because of the cartels. Personally, I don't care what they do. We just want to be left alone to practice our faith. We did not know if you were part of a cartel, coming to attack us." He carefully watched the men's reactions.

The old man continued, "I am sorry. I think your friend was killed by one of the cartels. We heard many shots the other night. They came from far away up the road. It sounded like a battle between two factions. We kept watch all night, but no one came here."

Nodding to one of the other men, the old man turned back to Jake. "You must leave now. My men will escort you back to the main road, and return your weapons there." He turned and walked back to the room to the left. Turning back, he said to the four men. "Never return here, or our welcome will not so understanding."

The men pushed Jake, Frank and Vega's men back outside. They cut the zip ties and waited while the four men got back into their vehicles. They then followed them back down the two track road in an old green pickup truck. When they reached the end of the road, the men threw the weapons into the back of the two vehicles. They closed the bushes behind them and disappeared.

Frank said, "That went well."

They spent the next two days going up and down the road, looking for Lucas. They finally gave up. Jake said, "There is nothing more we can do. The trail has gone cold." The Director's words rang inside his head. *We don't leave soldiers behind.*

Chapter 12 The Warehouse; 3 Weeks Earlier

"I'm not leaving Posadas until we find Lucas," Jake said.

Returning to the warehouse, Jake called the Director. Jake had to hold the phone away from his ear during the ten-minute tirade. When the call was over, Frank looked at him and asked, "Now what?"

"The Director ordered that we continue working with Vega, supposedly against the cartels, and continue gathering intel."

Jake knew that Vega was dirty, and he also knew that the other cartels were worse. Without looking at Frank, he said, "It is better to work with the devil you know."

Chapter 13

The Sorcerer's Apprentice

Lucas awakened to near blackness. A small kerosene lantern was flickering on the table from across the room. Its light was reflected from the cold metal walls of the Arcum Deus, casting a yellowish glow. Hearing a cacophony of breathing and muffled snoring, Lucas sat up slowly, scanning the room. Checking his watch, the luminescent dial confirmed what he already knew; it was 5:00 am. Slipping out of his sleeping bag liner, he stood up. He was wearing only his socks. A brown robe was neatly folded at the base of his sleeping bag. Feeling the chill of the underground air, he squirmed into the robe. Stepping gingerly around the sleeping men, he padded over to the table.

His pack was leaning against the wall, in the middle of a line of similar backpacks. Several large duffle bags were lined up to the left. Reaching into his pack, he found his water bottle and drained it into his parched throat. As soon as the cool water reached his stomach, his body announced a pressing need. Scanning the room, he could find nothing suitable for his purposes. Reaching into his pack, he found his compact headlamp. Pushing the button until the lights turned red, his slipped the strap over his forehead. Walking back down the lava tube, he searched for a suitable place to relive himself. Then he saw it. Fifty yards down the tube, someone had set up a portable commode. *They think of everything.*

173

Chapter 13   The Sorcerer's Apprentice

Afterwards, walking back toward the Arcum Deus, Lucas stopped halfway. He removed his headlamp and set it on the cold molten floor, aiming the beam toward the center of the tube. It gave him just enough light. He ran through his exercise routine until he was out of breath. Sitting down, he turned off his headlamp, closed his eyes, and let his mind process the events of the last few days.

He had to admit to himself that Hanz was not delusional. Knowing that was true, he had to accept the reality that something outside of his fund of scientific knowledge was going on. There was some ancient body of knowledge that had been hidden from him, and from generations of scientists. What he had seen last night overturned all the current scientific beliefs about space, time, and even gravity. One thing was true. He had to learn more.

Hearing a soft scraping on the floor, he opened his eyes. Someone was coming from the Arca. Switching his headlamp to red, he saw Santiago walking toward him.

"May I sit with you?" Santiago asked.

Lucas nodded and watched carefully, as the tall man gracefully lowered himself to the floor next to him.

Santiago sighed and said, "It is a lot to take in, I know."

"What do you know, really? How does that room function? How in the world does it transfer matter and energy across hundreds of miles with no visible power source? Who made it?"

Santiago held up a hand. "I have asked all of those questions, Lucas, and I am still questioning. I have been through all of the ancient writings I could find. There are tales, legends, speculation, and yes, even delusional thinking. Our western science does not explain it, but there are so many gaps in our scientific knowledge of the universe and its laws, that perhaps a theory can someday be developed, based on this new information. Perhaps if your Einstein had seen the Arcum, the world would be a different place. But, as he found out with the atomic bomb, different isn't always better."

"Knowledge is power, "Lucas said, "but power corrupts."

"Exactly. That is why we and our forbearers wisely chose to keep this a secret from the world. The Brujos Blanco have always been a force for good, fighting against evil whenever we could." Santiago looked down at his sandals.

"It sounds like there is a something you are worried about," Lucas said.

"Oh, I worry about many things, Lucas. I am worried about you, for example. You are a westerner, trained in western science. You have loyalty to your country, and I can respect that. But your country cannot learn about the Arca. They thought they were using the atomic bomb for good, but they could not keep it out of the hands of evil men. That knowledge and that power may destroy us all one day. I worry about what will happen if the secrets of the Arca get out."

"You do not know if you can trust me, is that it?"

Santiago turned and looked into Lucas' eyes. Lucas felt the power of the man, his wisdom, and his sadness. He sensed that Santiago was carrying a heavy burden, and had experienced some great loss. Was it the loss of a person, or the loss of his own innocence?

Looking away, Santiago said, "No. I do not know if I can trust you. But, I will find out soon enough during your training. We will begin this morning."

***

Hanz and Santiago outlined the apprenticeship Lucas would endure. The training would be abbreviated, because Lucas had already mastered many of the physical and combat skills. He still needed to learn control over his pain and his fear. They trained for many days inside the Arcum room. He learned about how to generate different vibrations for different purposes, and how to activate the passageway to another Arcum. He was not allowed to travel though passageway, as that would be part of his final training.

They left the lava tube many times to go into the mountainside and the surrounding desert. He learned about the many plants with medicinal and hallucinogenic properties. Some plants could be used to cause, or to ease, pain and suffering. Others could cause men to tell the truth. None of them were without potentially dangerous side-effects.

Early in the morning of the third day in the third week, Santiago was standing over Lucas when he awakened at his usual time. The man was wearing a parka over his robe. He motioned for Lucas to follow him. Throwing on his robe and parka, Lucas slipped into his sandals and followed Santiago down the lava tube to the entrance.

Stepping outside the round door, he saw that it was still dark. Dawn was a few hours away. The stars were brilliant and gave them sufficient light to navigate safely. They scrambled around the side of the volcano and climbed upward to a barren shelf overlooking the valley below. Sitting down, they enjoyed the view together in silence for several minutes.

Santiago reached into his pouch and produced a small vile of liquid. "We will drink this so that you may find your spirit animal. It is dangerous, but I will be here with you to guide you."

Lucas took the vial and asked, "What is it?"

Chapter 13   The Sorcerer's Apprentice

"It is a mixture of two of the plants you have been studying. They are brugmansia, or angel's trumpet, and chacruna; which will help your body absorb the mixture. It is the mixture that allows you to open your soul, and it brings to you your spirit animal or guide. Unfortunately, it can also bring your spirit enemy. You may have to battle with the enemy to join with your guide. You will have to use all that we have taught you, or you may end up leaving this mountain in madness."

"And you want me to drink this?" Lucas thought that it was one thing to study these plants, but it was altogether another thing to actually ingest them.

"I don't want you to do anything," Santiago replied. "I am offering you a way to move into the spirit world. It is a part of becoming a Brujo Blanco. You do not have to do this. If you choose to refuse, that is acceptable to us. We will go back inside the Arca and we will remove all memories of this place from your mind."

"You can do that?"

"Yes, we can do that. You will then awaken in a few days, and you will be back in the jungle outside of Posada. You will not know how you got there and you will have a terrible headache, but you will otherwise be fine physically and mentally."

"When do I have to decide?"

"You may decide now, or take the day to think about it. We can do this again, tomorrow morning. After tomorrow, I must go back to Mexico and the rest of you must go back to the fortress sanctuary to continue your training."

The vial glistened in Lucas fingers. He had been exposed to various mind-altering drugs as part of his training to learn to resist interrogations. The training was designed to shatter one's reality and to make one susceptible to suggestion. They were horrible, disorienting experiences.

"I think I will take the day to consider my choice."

Santiago smiled, his eyes twinkling in the star light. "Yes, I thought so. I made the same choice myself, many years ago."

"But then you did it? You drank the solution?"

"Well, I am a Brujo Blanco," Santiago replied.

Standing up, Lucas handed the vial to Santiago. "I think I will take a long walk now. I will see you back inside the Arcum."

Santiago took the vial and placed it back inside his pouch. He stood and started walking slowly back to the lava tube.

Lucas walked around the volcano for many hours. When the sun emerged over the top of the distant mountains, he performed the ending of his exercise routine, the salute to the sun. He then returned to the Arcum. He had many more questions that needed answering.

***

The pain in his head was unbearable. Lucas could barely open his eyes as the morning light felt like red hot needles poking into his retinas. Feeling with his hands, he sensed wet grass and a rocky soil underneath him. His left hand brushed against some rough fabric. Moving closer, he realized that it was his pack. Fumbling with the straps, he was finally able to open it and feel around inside for his water bottles. Finding one, he opened it and gulped a half liter before gasping for air. Lying back down, he waited for the pain to subside. He could not gather his thoughts. It felt like his brains were scrambled. He estimated that it took almost an hour before he could sit up again. It might have been five minutes. *What is wrong with me?*

He could now open his eyes just a little wider. Reaching inside the pack, he found his radio. Lifting it out of the pack, memories started to return in flashes. *We were on a mission. Vega, Jake, and who were those other people? A fire fight. Wine, steak, some tents. No, two fire fights. Wait, I was shot.*

Lucas reached down to his side. There was not any pain. Forcing his eyes open wider, despite the pain in his eyes, he lifted his shirt. *Where did I get this shirt?*

Where are my fatigues? There was no wound. *I must have been dreaming. Was it another nightmare? Where am I?*

Lucas finished the rest of the water in the bottle. He found another full bottle in his pack. Opening a small pocket on the side of the pack, he found a small metal tin containing aspirin. He popped three into his mouth and drank some more water.

He sat there for a long time, trying to knit his memories back together. *There was a firefight. We were fighting with Vega. We found bundles of drugs. There was a camp. We ate. Then we were attacked, and yes, I was shot.* He checked his side again. There was still no evidence of a wound.

The aspirin started to kick in. Looking around, he saw that he was sitting on top of a ridge. There was a city below. *Is that Posadas? Where is Jake? How did I get here? What am I doing up here?*

Staring at the radio for several minutes, Lucas finally pushed some buttons and lifted the radio to his mouth. "Jake? Do you copy?"

Chapter 13　The Sorcerer's Apprentice

Chapter 14

Reunion

Frank jumped when the slightly garbled voice came through the radio. "Jake? Do you Copy? Jake?"

Jake said, "What the hell?" He snatched the radio off of the dashboard. Pressing the talk button, he answered, "Who is this?"

"Jake. It's me, Jake. Lucas."

Frank pulled off to the side of the road. Shaking his head at Jake, he said, "Hold on. It's gotta be a trap."

"Trap or not. It sounds like Lucas." Jake thought a moment and then pressed the button. "If you are Lucas, tell me what kind of soda does Frank drink?"

Frank looked at him quizzically. After a few moments, the voice came back, "Frank doesn't drink soda. He drinks Malbec with garlic."

Frank smiled and grabbed the radio, "Lucas. It's me Frank. Are you okay? Where are you?"

Lucas answered, "I'm not sure. I am on some ridge overlooking what I think is Posadas to my left. Yes, it is Posadas. I can see the bridge to Paraguay. I'm sitting next to a dirt road that leads down into the valley."

Frank practically screamed into the radio. "Stay where you are, we are on our way. We should be there in twenty minutes."

Frank drove like a race-car driver and made it there in ten minutes. Jake hung on for dear life the whole way.

The Suburban was still rolling when Jake jumped out of the door and ran over to Lucas, who was sitting under a tree.

"Jesus, Lucas. What happened to you? Where have you been? What are you wearing? How are you feeling? Where have you been? Jesus, Lucas. We thought you were dead. Where did you go?"

Lucas smiled and then started laughing. The pain knifed back into his eyes and he grabbed his head and groaned.

Frank said, "Whoa, Jake. Slow down. Don't you remember? He's been shot."

Lucas looked at him and his eyes widened. "Shot? Did you say I was shot? I remember being shot, but then I thought it was a nightmare."

Frank said, "It was no nightmare, you egghead. Let me take a look. It might be infected."

Lucas raised his shirt and watched the two men's faces change from concern to bewilderment.

"What the…" Frank reached out and touched Lucas' side. "Where's the hole?" Lifting Lucas' shirt, he looked around to Lucas' back. He glanced up at Lucas' face, and then looked at Jake, who just stood there, now speechless, with his mouth open.

Turning back to Lucas, Frank muttered, "I patched you up. You lost a lot of blood. Man, I thought you were going to die."

Frank stood up and started backing away. "What's going on here?"

Lucas shook his head. "I don't know. I really do not know. All I remember is that late last night, we were at Vega's camp, and we were attacked."

Jake finally closed his mouth and stared at Lucas. He finally said, "Lucas, that wasn't last night. That was over six weeks ago."

"Six weeks ago? What's wrong with you guys? That was last night," Lucas insisted.

"It was six weeks ago, and you were shot, shot bad. We both saw it."

Frank broke the tension, saying, "Whatever. You're here now, and you're alive. That's all I care about. We're too much in the open here. Let's go back to the warehouse and we can sort it out there."

Lucas looked at Frank and asked, "Warehouse? What warehouse?"

Frank replied, "Oh, we have a nice warehouse now. We also have this big beautiful four wheel drive, bullet proof SUV. It has air conditioning. Now let's get you inside."

The two men helped Lucas over to the SUV. He started to get into the back seat, but Frank stopped him. "Oh no. You're taking shotgun. I want to keep an eye on you so that you don't disappear again." They helped him into the front seat and Jake climbed into the back. Once everyone was inside, Frank locked the doors.

Frank drove very carefully, almost slowly, back to the warehouse. He kept looking over at Lucas, who was just squinting out through the windows.

Jake started asking more questions, but Lucas waved him off. His head was still hurting like the worst hangover. He could not keep his eyes open without the stabbing pain returning. Feeling nauseated, he sipped some more water and took slow deep breaths.

After a few minutes, he said, "Fill me in on what happened, after I...after I disappeared."

Jake recounted the story, starting with driving into the jungle with Vega and his men. Every once in a while, Frank interjected, adding to the story with his own observations. Lucas listened, trying to fill in the blanks of his memory. The last thing he remembered was lying on the ground after being shot, and Frank trying to stop the bleeding. He could recall nothing after that. It was as if he had died and was suddenly reborn at the top of the ridge.

Frank had insisted that he could not have left the back of the truck on his own. Someone must have taken him, but they did not know who, or how. Lucas began to feel angry and violated. Losing an hour in a blackout was one thing, and that could be a frightening experience. It was another thing to lose over six weeks.

After arriving at the warehouse, the first thing Lucas did was to take a shower. The hot water helped the pain diminish, and he let the liquid flow over his head and face for many minutes. Deciding to eliminate some possibilities, he slowly and methodically examined his body, looking for any signs of trauma or violation. There were no needle marks that would suggest he had been drugged. There were no signs of torture. His faced had been shaved recently. He could find no answers.

He tried to focus his mind, to recall anything, any small detail, faces, sounds, smells, but it was all a blank. He thought maybe he had been unconscious, in a coma or something. Then he noted that his muscles had not lost their tone, concluding that he must have exercised during the lost weeks. He had not been unconscious during that time. He was troubled the most by having no scar or signs that he had been shot.

That made no sense, especially since Frank and Jake confirmed that he had been shot and the bullet went through him. He should have wounds on both sides.

Stepping out of the shower and drying off, he could smell bacon cooking. Someone left a fresh set of clothes in the bathroom, and he quickly dressed. He could keep his eyes open without the lightning bolts of pain.

Entering the small kitchen, he noticed Jake was looking at him suspiciously. The mini-split AC unit was blowing on high. Frank was standing next to the stove, cooking eggs and whistling quietly to himself. Lucas tried to pick out the tune. It sounded like the Bee Gees song, Stayin' Alive. Frank turned his head at Lucas' arrival.

"Well, back from the dead, Lazarus," he said. He looked at Lucas, scanning him from head to toe for a moment before turning back to his eggs.

Jakes scowled at the back of Frank's head, and then asked, "How are you feeling, Lucas? Anything come back to you?"

Lucas didn't answer right away. He stood there, slightly dropping his shoulders and shaking his head. He had never felt so disoriented, so out of control of his own mind. What he did know, was that the bacon was beckoning to his stomach. Pulling out a chair, he sat down at the table across from Jake. He noted that both men were armed, and he was not.

"Where is my sidearm?" he asked.

Jake replied, "I left it in the SUV. It was in your pack, along with the rest of your kit. Only the water bottles had been touched. I washed them out and refilled them for you. I couldn't find your fatigues." He did not offer to get Lucas' gun.

Lucas noted that Jake was not smiling and there was some tension in his face and body. He was coiled, ready to strike at a second's notice. Lucas' mind kicked into gear.

He said, "I know what you are thinking, Jake. You are wondering if I was captured by the enemy, and you are thinking that they brainwashed me. You are wondering if I am some kind of Manchurian Candidate. You are wondering if, at any moment, I am going to snap and kill the president. That is why I am unarmed, and you are not."

Jake did not reply, and he did not relax.

Frank turned, holding the spatula in his hand, floating in the air. He looked back and forth between Jake and Lucas. "Jake. What the hell? This is Lucas."

Lucas continued, "No Frank. It is okay. I would be thinking the same thing. Occam's Razor: The simplest explanation is usually the correct one. Or, to be more precise: Among competing hypotheses, the one with the fewest assumptions should be selected."

Frank turned to Jake, "You see? You hear that? That's the Lucas we know."

Jake did not change his expression but said, "Let's eat." He still did not relax. He kept sitting on the edge of his chair, his feet firmly planted on the floor underneath him.

Frank served Lucas first, and then plopped some more eggs on Jake's plate. He then handed out the bacon, but Lucas noted he received a few extra pieces from Frank. They ate together in silence.

When they were finished, Jake said, "You know, Lucas, we are going to have to call Director Triana. He is going to want to talk to you, most likely in person. Although, if I were him, I'd want you thoroughly examined first."

"Right. You better brief him first before I speak to him. Do you want me to leave the room?"

Jake replied, "I think that would be best."

Frank slammed some dishes into the sink, but made no other statement. Lucas got up and went outside. The surrounding area was mostly industrial, without the aesthetic landscaping seen downtown. It was heating up, and Lucas felt his skin getting moist. He began to imagine what he was going to tell the Director. He was beginning to feel hot inside his body.

This was his first mission, and he went AWOL for over six weeks. He suspected that this was not going to go well. *The Director might think we are all crazy, or we victims of some mass hysteria or, worse, that we are doing drugs or staying drunk down here. How is he going to trust us ever again?*

He wondered what his father would think about all of this. Would he be disappointed? He would certainly be disbelieving. Maybe he would be curious and look at this as an academic exercise, solving problems with too many unknown variables. Lucas' reverie was interrupted by the sound of the door opening. Jake was standing there with the sat phone held to his ear. He waved Lucas over.

Taking a deep breath, he quickly walked back to the doorway. Jake handed the phone to him as Lucas went back inside. Frank and Jake left the room, going into the garage, and closing the door behind them.

"Dr. Forge here."

Expecting the Director, he was surprised to hear Cecelia's voice, speaking softly, "Dr. Forge, are you alright?"

"I feel fine, Cecelia, I'm just mystified. Does the Director want to talk to me?"

"He does, Dr. Forge, but not right now. He wants you to come back here. A transport is leaving your airport in 4 hours. When you land here, you will be met on the tarmac. Report to medical when you arrive…and Dr. Forge? Do not take any detours."

"No, ma'am, I will come there directly."

"Good. I will let the Director know." She ended the call abruptly.

Lucas breathed a sigh of relieve. He knew that at least he had some time to gather his wits about him. He hoped that his memories of the past weeks would start to return so that he had some rational explanation. He cared more about that than having to defend himself to the Director.

Frank poked his head inside. He whispered, "Are you off the phone?"

"Yes. That was Cecelia. They want me to come back to Langley. I leave here in four hours."

"What about us?"

"I do not know. Maybe we should ask Jake."

Jake was sitting on one of the crates, staring at the wall. When Frank approached him, Jake stood up and said, "We have to secure this building and pack our kits. The Director wants all of us back there."

Lucas felt horrible. It was bad enough that he screwed things up, but now the men must be worried that their

192

own careers were on the line. He had to think of some way to absolve them of any blame. He owed them that. He owed them his life.

Chapter 14   Reunion

Chapter 15

Leaving Posadas

Frank started the engine as the garage door was opening. Lucas climbed into the front seat, while Jake moved his large bulk into the back. The diesel engine was loud, trapped inside the garage, the sounds vibrating off of the walls, Once everyone was secure, Frank pushed the accelerator and pulled out, pressing a remote to close the garage behind them. He made sure it was shut before pulling out into the road. Traffic was light, so he accelerated rapidly.

Lucas watched the road ahead and to the right ninety degrees. The mood in the vehicle was somber, pressing down on the men like a heavy blanket. Jake had swiveled around, and was watching the rear, his trigger finger straight against the receiver on his rifle. Lucas was still unarmed, which both irritated him and made him feel vulnerable.

He asked, "Did you get any valuable intel from Vega while I was…gone?"

Frank answered, "He said he somehow confirmed that the men we ambushed were part of the Mendoza Mafia, who recently joined forces with some group that manufactures the drugs. I don't know if I believe anything he says."

"The Mendoza Mafia is pretty far from home. What are they doing up here?"

"Apparently, they have small groups stationed strategically near various border crossings. The drug manufacturers have stepped up production to meet the heavy demand from the US. They have heavy muscle, and provide protection to the runners."

Jake added, "We think that the group that attacked us was part of that heavy muscle. They are well armed and well financed. They buy a lot of influence with the local police and governments."

Lucas replied, "So they are getting bigger and smarter."

Jake said, "They are a lot smarter. They are also buying up some of the local papers and bribing the radio stations. The media has started to portray them as local heroes, robbing America and spreading the proceeds among the locals down here."

Lucas said, "I'm guessing they are prohibiting the sale and use of their drugs on this side of the border?"

Jake answered, "Yeah. One of the local drug dealers ended up floating in the river, with his severed head hanging from an overpass downtown. It hung there for a week until someone cut it down. It sent a strong message."

"So Vega has been going after the runners, not going after the bigger fish?"

Frank glanced at Lucas. "What are you getting at?"

Lucas thought a moment. "The drug runners are at the bottom of the rung. They are a dime a dozen. They probably recruit poor kids or petty criminals to act as their mules. Vega takes out a few of them here and there, and he looks like he is doing something. The government puts him on a pedestal and they can tout that they are making major inroads into the drug trafficking problem. Meanwhile, the big fish are barely affected."

Frank asked, "So Vega is in on it?"

Lucas answered, "I'm pretty sure Vega is a psychopath, or more accurately, he is a person with Antisocial Personality Disorder. He has no morals, no empathy, and no fear. He probably enjoys killing the mules. He enjoys the respect given to him by the Government. He enjoys the con game. He is like a sanctioned murderer. It wouldn't surprise me that he is tipped off where to find the mules, while the big shipments are made elsewhere."

Jake asked, "So why were we attacked at the camp. Weren't those cartel assassins?"

Lucas asked, "Did either of you check the duffel bags for drugs?"

Frank and Jake both shook their heads 'no'.

Lucas continued, "I'm thinking that there were no drugs in those bags. Vega set up the supposed drug runners, his own men, and us at the same time. He escapes being killed, and that makes him an even bigger hero that almost got killed doing his job."

Frank said, "Son of a bitch. He played us."

Suddenly, the windshield was hit by three loud percussions. The sound was deafening. Saucer size cracks appeared like spider webs in the bullet proof glass.

"Incoming!" yelled Frank as he made sharp evasive maneuvers on the two lane road.

"Give me a rifle," Lucas shouted toward Jake, while trying to spot the shooter.

Jake hesitated, still not sure if he could trust Lucas.

Two more bullets hit the side windows, and they could hear a dozen more impacts hit the passenger side doors.

Hanging on to the dashboard with one hand, Lucas turned to Jake, "I saw muzzle flashes from the overpass. Give me a rifle." More bullets hit Frank's window and he swerved hard to the right.

"Shit. Okay, here." Jake said, handing his rifle to Lucas. "The Director said to keep you unarmed. Sorry Lucas."

"The Director isn't here," Lucas answered, checking the chamber and magazine. He rolled down his window a few inches and pointed toward the overpass. "Hold it steady, Frank." A moment later he said, "Jake. Spot me."

Finding his target, Lucas shot five times in two seconds. His ears started ringing from the loud explosions of the 5.56 mm ammunition. Jake yelled, "Tango down. Tango down," as he grabbed another rifle from the seat. Frank swerved to the left.

Six more rounds struck Frank's door. "Shit! He's on the roof of that gas station on the left. Ten o'clock."

Jake cracked his window and lined up his sights. "Steady, Frank." Pausing for several seconds, and switching to burst mode, he pressed the trigger, just as another three rounds hit his window. "Did I get him?"

"I can't tell, but he's not there anymore," Lucas answered.

Frank yelled, "Six o'clock. Two men on a motorcycle."

Jake spun around and looked out the back window. Two men were on a large motorcycle, wearing black leather, and black helmets. They were gaining on them fast. The passenger was pointing a small machine pistol at the back of the SUV. Lucas kept scanning ahead and to his right. The motorcycle banked to the right and started to pull along side of the SUV. A burst of bullets hit the side of the Suburban.

Lucas said, "Unlock the doors, Frank." Spinning to his right, he heard the door locks click open. The motorcycle was pulling closer. The passenger aimed his pistol at Jake's window, inches away from the glass, and fired a long burst. Jake's window turned opaque from the impact.

Kicking open his door, Lucas yelled, "Frank, Slam on the brakes." The tires screamed, and the motorcycle hit the door, sending the two men over the top. The riderless motorcycle held steady for a few seconds before falling over and bouncing along the road. The two men tumbled and rolled akimbo on the asphalt. Lucas poured several rounds into each of the men as the SUV passed by.

Lucas tried to close his door, but it was badly warped from the impact of the motorcycle. It would not lock shut. Reaching a hand back toward Jake, he said, "Reload." Without hesitating, Jake handed him another magazine. Keeping his eyes on the road ahead, Lucas released the used magazine from the rifle and replaced it with the fresh one. He checked the chamber with his trigger finger, and raised the rifle to the ready position. "Everybody okay?" he asked.

"I'm okay," they said in unison.

"How far to the airport?" asked Jake.

Frank answered, "About ten minutes." He added, "Or a lifetime."

They continued without incident and pulled into the secured section, far from the main terminal. Frank checked his watch. "The plane should be here in a few minutes."

They stayed inside the SUV, keeping watch in all directions. Five minutes later, a flat gray executive jet taxied up nearby. The men waited until the hatch opened and a stairway dropped to the tarmac. Grabbing their packs, the men ran to the plane and climbed up the stairs. Jake yelled toward the pilot, "Go, go, go." The men strapped themselves in, and waited impatiently.

The stairway retracted and the hatch was sealed as the pilot turned the plane around. He spoke to the tower and a few seconds later, they were moving toward the runway. Within a minute, they were airborne.

Frank said, "Welcome to Posadas. Now Yankee go home." Ten minutes later, all three men were sound asleep.

Five hours later, Lucas woke up and spent a few seconds trying to remember where he was. Standing up, he made his way to the back of the plane and used the facilities. Lifting his shirt, he checked again where a wound should have been. There was no trace of an injury. Sitting down near the rear of the plane, he again tried to regain his memories. He still drew a blank.

Looking out the small window, he saw that the plane was flying above a solid sheet of clouds. He surmised that they must be over some Caribbean islands, and part of him wished that he was sitting on a beach below, sipping an umbrella drink.

He was dreading returning to Langley and felt his anxiety rise. Forcing his mind to examine his thoughts, he began identifying a set of 'what if' statements that were fueling his anxiety. He challenged and disputed those statements, taking them to the worst case scenarios. Satisfied that he could handle those possibilities, he felt his anxiety diminish.

Hearing some noises coming from the front of the plane, he leaned out over the aisle. A flight attendant was busy in her mini kitchen. Walking up to her, he asked, "Do you have anything to read?"

She smiled, and pointed to an open overhead bin containing a stack of magazines. Flipping through a pile of brainless celebrity and fashion mags, he found a recent Scientific American and took it back to his seat. He immersed himself in an article by some fellow named Stephen Hawking, writing about quantum mechanics. He finished the article as the plane was making its final approach.

Just as Cecelia told him, they were met on the tarmac by several men in dark suits, wearing dark sunglasses, even though the sun was setting. The men were standing next to two black Suburbans and one of the men motioned them over. As soon as they got to the vehicles, one of the men frisked them, relieving them of their side arms, knives, and multitools.

Within an hour, they were pulling into Langley. They were met by an identical set of men in dark suits who escorted them to the medical facility.

The three were separated and Lucas was taken to a small interview room. He waited an hour before anyone showed up. The man who finally arrived was a short, bespectacled, balding man who was carelessly dressed in a patterned blazer and tan pants. Even Lucas could tell that the pattern of his tie clashed with his blazer. Behind his thick glasses, his bright eyes revealed a formidable intellect. He was carrying a thick folder that he placed on the table in front of him and then he sat down. Pulling a small recorder from his pocket, he pressed the record button. He did not ask permission.

"Dr. Forge, I presume? He began in a reedy voice. "I have some questions for you, but first I want you to tell me, in your own words, what transpired in Posadas, Argentina during the last month. Lucas decided that there was no point in trying to deceive or embellish, so he presented the facts as he knew them. The interview took over three hours.

He was then escorted to another room, which was a medical exam room. They had him switch to a flimsy, open-backed hospital gown, printed with a faded blue design. He had to give up several vials of blood, a cup of urine, and was poked, prodded, and x-rayed for several more hours. He was moved to another room where they performed an EKG, EEG, and a treadmill test. He was thoroughly exhausted.

Asking if he could go home, he was told that he was being admitted for an overnight observation. He was shown to a private room with a hospital bed. An attendant came in and placed another set of EEG electrodes on his scalp. EKG sensors were stuck to his chest, a blood pressure cup was slipped over his arm, and a sensor with a red light was clipped over his finger.
He noticed that there was a camera attached to the corner of the ceiling. The attendant told him to go to sleep. Lucas tried, but he was awakened every hour by a nurse or technician taking his vitals or checking his wiring harnesses.

In the morning, he had to give more blood and urine. The sensors were removed from his scalp and chest. A large woman in a white uniform brought in a tray containing a tasteless breakfast, with watered down coffee. When she returned to remove the tray, he asked if they had any green Jello. She gave him a dirty look and walked out.

There was nothing to read and there was no television in the windowless, barren room. Lucas walked over to the door and found that it was locked. Removing the gown, Lucas pushed through his exercise routine for the next hour. Lying down on the bed, he tried to remember passages from Marcus Aurelius' writings. Nothing else happened for several hours.

Finally, the door opened and an attendant brought in a padded chair. He was followed by the same balding, bespectacled man who interviewed him yesterday. He seemed to be wearing the same outfit he had on the day before. The man sat down and turned on his recorder. He then proceeded to ask him the exact same questions for the next three hours.

He asked the man if he could have something to read. The man looked sad, and shook his head, saying, "Sorry." When the man left, the attendant returned and removed the chair. Before he left, Lucas asked him if he could get something to read. The man looked up at the camera, and shook his head, 'no'.

Lucas busied himself counting the tiles in the floor, the tiles in the ceiling, and the tiles in the bathroom. He was about to start pounding on the door, when a man in a white uniform brought him a set of clothes, and set them on the bed before leaving.

Lucas removed his gown and dressed himself in the Khaki pants, a navy blue polo shirt, white socks and sneakers. He was surprised to find they were all in his correct size. He started to sit on the bed, when two men in dark suits entered the room and escorted him out into the hall. They walked though several sets of guarded secure doors and got into an elevator. One of the men pushed the button for the second floor. When the doors opened, they turned right and walked through another guarded entrance. They came to another set of elevators, and climbed to the fifth floor. When the doors opened, he recognized the Director's office lobby.

Cecelia looked up and seemed surprised at Lucas' appearance. She pressed a button on her desk and announced, "Sir, Dr. Forge is here." She buzzed him through.

Lucas entered the office and saw Jake Holstein standing next to the desk in his usual position. He walked up to the desk and stood at attention.

Director Triana questioned him from behind the desk for the next thirty minutes. He then stood up and walked over to the windows and stared at the trees for several more minutes. He finally turned back, and again sat in his large leather chair.

"I don't know what to do with you, Forge. I don't like not knowing what to do with people. Neither you, nor anyone else, can tell me what happened to you during the six weeks you were missing."

Looking down at the file on his desk, he continued, "The neurologist thinks that you might have become anoxic after being shot. The internist says you were never shot. The psychologists think you were all drugged and had the same hallucination. In the end, they all gave you two and Frank a clean bill of health."

He stared at Lucas, while his finger drummed on top of his desk. "Jake says you are okay and that you may have saved his life during two ambushes. He says he'll serve with you anywhere and anytime."

Lucas stole a glance at Jake. Holstein stared straight ahead, his face without expression.

The Director leaned forward and put his elbows on the desk. He steepled his fingers in front of his mouth and looked back and forth between Jake and Lucas. "I may regret this, but I am putting you back into the field. I want you to take a week off first. Forge, if you change your mind about this work, just let Cecelia know. Now, both of you get out of here."

Chapter 15 Leaving Posadas

Chapter 16

The Ledger

The phone rang three times before Lucas could get to it. "Forge here," he answered.

A deep, raspy voice on the other end said, "Dr. Forge? I don't know if you remember me. I'm Detective Lindsay from the Sheriff's office."

"Detective Lindsay, of course I remember you. How are you doing?"

"I am doing just great. Remember that case you helped me with?"

"Yes I do. The serial killer."

"Well, we got him."

"You did? That is terrific. How did you find him?

"As you suggested, we staked out several of the arroyos, and sure enough after a month, he showed up. He put up quite a fight, swinging that shovel of his at the deputies."

"So, you got him then. Did he confess?"

"We didn't give him a chance, him swinging that shovel at us and all. He ended up with about six bullet holes in his chest. It was a nice grouping. We called the ambulance, and by the time they got there, about three hours later, the perp was dead and cold. Damn shame, if you catch my drift."

"Yes, I see. It is too bad about that."

"We searched his house, quite a nice mansion up in Troon. We found some interesting items. I thought you might want to take a look."

"Indeed I would, Detective. Where should I go?"

Detective Lindsay gave him the directions, and they made arrangements to meet later that afternoon. Lucas stopped by the library and continued his research into Argentine history and topography. His curiosity often took him esoteric directions, and he could spend hours learning about little known topics. This time, he was initially searching for leads about addictive or hallucinogenic drugs. He thought that maybe he could find something that would explain his lost six weeks.

He found a few chapters describing ancient healing ceremonies practiced by a secretive cast of shaman known as the Kallawaya, also known as Callahuaya. He was intrigued, learning that individual Kallawayas knew the medical properties of over nine hundred different plant species; a knowledge that is passed from father to son. Some of the authors credited the Kallawayas with being the first to use the dried bark of the cinchona tree, the source of **quinine**, to prevent and cure malaria. For many centuries, the Kallawayas

210

wandered through the Andes, from Bolivia, to Paraguay, and down into Argentina, collecting herbs and performing ritualistic ceremonies.

In one of the books, he found photos and illustrations of some of the plants. He had a nagging feeling that something about one of the plants was familiar, yet he knew he had never seen it before. Turning to another book, he found that the Kallawaya medicine men spoke a secret tongue known as Machaj Juyay. Some of researchers believed Machaj Juyay is related to the secret language spoken in private by the Inca ruling elite.

Digging deeper, he found that in 1970, archeologists uncovered a skeleton in the Charazani valley which had been buried with recognizable Kallawaya paraphernalia. This was carbon-dated to between 800 and 1000 BC, two thousand years before the rise of the Inca Empire. He could find nothing about a memory erasing substance.

Looking at his watch, he realized that if he didn't hurry, he would be late for his meeting with the detective. Stuffing his notes into his briefcase, he hurried out to his vehicle. Even though he had parked in the shade, the temperature inside was well over 120 degrees. He opened two of the doors to let out some of the heat while starting the engine, and turning on the AC.

Troon was a new developing luxury community in Scottsdale Arizona. The plans were for multi-acre lots and a golf course country club. The surrounding area was open desert, with majestic saguaro cacti, palo verde trees, and mesquite bushes. Jackrabbits darted in and out of the bushes, foraging for food in the desolate landscape. Lucas spotted the detective's white SUV parked in front of a large mansion that appeared as if it had erupted out of the desert. Yellow police tape was still hanging on the doorway.

Knocking on the front door, Lucas marveled at the high arched entranceway and the large ornate pots lining the portal. They contained decaying flowers. Detective Lindsay opened the door and ushered Lucas inside.

The home was professionally decorated in nouveau riche decadence. Lindsay pointed him to a set of large wooden doors to the left. The heavy doors opened into an enormous study, displaying floor to ceiling bookshelves, packed with mostly leather bound volumes.

The detective walked over to a massive wooden desk with an open file folder lying on its highly polished surface. Inside the folder was a worn ledger. "I wanted you to see this before it gets buried in an evidence locker."

Lucas took the ledger and began perusing its contents. The writing was neat and precise, almost feminine. It was a record of meeting times and places, complete with names, addresses, and phone numbers. The writer had added comments about each of the names, including physical descriptions, tastes in wine and cigars, personality traits, estimated financial worth, and even sexual proclivities.

Lucas said, "He was profiling these people, albeit in a crude fashion."

"Look at the second section, past the yellow tab."

Lucas found the tab and opened the pages. There were more names and profiles. Then he spotted it. The names were all from south of the US border.

The detective said, "Given your work, I thought you might like of copy of this." He was smiling, knowingly.

Lucas studied his face, wondering how much the detective knew about his work with the agency.

Seeing the look on Lucas' face, he said, "Look, you don't have to tell me the details of what you do. I probably don't want to know anyway. If I did, you'd have to kill me, right?"

Without waiting for a response, he continued. "You did me a favor, and I just thought I would return the favor. You don't have to take it."

Reading through the list of names, Luca knew that there was a goldmine of valuable information contained in those pages. The Director would be very interested. Lucas did not want to let the detective know just how interested, so he tried to act nonchalant.

"This looks interesting. Maybe some of the names will turn out to be leads. It's not my area, so I will pass it along through the proper channels. Thank you. Maybe I will get a gold star from my boss."

"Well, I hope so." He pulled out a large envelope. "I already made the copies in case you wanted them." He handed the envelope to Lucas and winked. "Good hunting."

When Lucas returned to his home outside of Wickenburg, the first thing he did was pick up the phone. He dialed a DC number. It was ten o'clock, Washington time, and he hoped Jake would still be awake.

"Yeah?" a groggy voice answered.

Lucas knew it was Jake and said, "I am coming back to DC tomorrow. I am bringing you a present."

Jake perked up, "Is she a red head?"

"No. It is something even better. We are back in business. Call Frank."

The next evening, Lucas walked into their designated bar. It was nearly empty on a Thursday night. Jake and Frank were sitting at the large booth in the rear. Jake was drinking beer out of a bottle, and Frank was nursing a pint glass of Guinness as usual. Seeing Lucas, Frank gave him a slight smile, and nudged Jake.

Lucas caught the eye of the sleepy bartender and said, "Jameson 18, neat please." The bartender pulled a bottle off the top shelf, and poured two fingers into a chilled glass.

Sliding into the booth next to Frank, Lucas greeted them with, "Gentlemen."

Frank said, "Nice place you picked. A real swinging joint."

Lucas said, "It is private and quiet, just as I like it. Hello Jake."

Jake looked around, and with a disappointed look, said, "I see you forgot the red head."

"I told you I had something better." He spent the next five minutes giving them the background on the serial killer.

Jake said, "Serial killers are not in our charter. Why are you telling us this?"

"Because," handing them copies of the ledger, "The killer had connections to the drug trade in Mexico, Central and South America. We have names, addresses, phone numbers, and even crude profiles on each of them. Take a look."

While the two were reading through the documents, Lucas went back to the bar and bought another round. He felt like celebrating tonight. A part of him wanted to redeem himself with the Director, but a larger part wanted to cut the heads off the snakes and make a real difference in their mission.

The men spent the next hour going over potential strategies. They wanted to be fully prepared when they met with the Director in the morning. Despite their excitement, the three men slept well that night.

The next morning, Lucas and Jake kept their appointment with Director Triana. It was supposed to last five minutes. After seeing the ledger, and listening to Jake's presentation, the Director told Cecelia to reschedule his next appointments and hold his calls.

***

It was Monday afternoon when the chartered jet landed in Puerto Penasco, Mexico. Lucas had arrangements to meet with some local contact, and begin setting up a network to track the main players in the drug trade. Jake and Frank were on their way to Mendoza, Argentina. The intel suggested that there was a major player who was taking over the mid-level players and creating an empire stretching across the continent.

Lucas exited the jet and walked toward the small building next to the single strip runway. A rugged man in worn jeans, a faded blue shirt, and wearing a white cowboy hat, approached him, holding out his hand. "Dr. Forge, I presume?" he asked, in flawless English.

Expecting to be speaking to a Mexican local, Lucas was momentarily off balance. He could only muster "Yes."

"Excellent. My name is José Montoya, and I will be your guide." The man winked at him conspiratorially. "Let's get your luggage."

The man lifted the duffle bag and put it in the back of a white Ford pickup truck. He slipped Lucas' carry-on bag behind the front seat. "I am taking you to my Hacienda. Are you hungry?"

Lucas had to admit that he was hungry. It had been six hours since he had eaten breakfast. "Actually, I'm famished. I do not want to be any trouble."

"Trouble? Oh no, you do not know my Maria. She loves to cook, and I must say, she is the best cook in Northern Mexico. She has been cooking all day in anticipation of your visit."

"I look forward to it."

While they were driving, José told him how he and Maria ran a sporting goods store, mostly for the tourists. Maria came from a wealthy family, but was bored with the society life in Mexico City, so they decided to move to Puerto Penasco, and start a more exciting life. She loved talking to the tourists and keeping life simple.

Lucas said, "If you don't mind my asking, how did you get involved with my company?"

José looked around, as if by habit, even though no one else was nearby. "I used to be in the Mexican Special Forces. I met some of your advisors, and they occasionally asked for my help. The pay was good, but I really did it for the adventure." He looked at Lucas carefully and added, "If you tell anyone I said that, I will have to kill you."

Lucas studied the man's face to see if he was serious. José burst out laughing and said, "I am only joking. I only kill bad guys, and I do not think you are a bad man. I can sense these things about people. But watch out for Maria. She is even more intuitive than I."

"Now you are frightening me. Maybe you should just drop me off at a hotel or something."

"If I do that, Maria will assassinate me. Do not worry, my new friend. Trust me that Maria will like you."

Soon, they pulled into a beautiful hacienda. It was obvious that they took pride in their property. The landscaping was lush and colorful. The house was painted in bright colors that would have been garish in the US, but down here, they were festive and inviting.

José pulled the duffle bag from the bed of the truck and walked Lucas inside his home. The scent of spicy beef and shrimp was intoxicating. José led Lucas into the kitchen, where a short women with long black hair, tied back with a ribbon, was stirring a large pot. She turned as the men entered her domain. She flashed a brilliant smile before José could speak.

"Maria, this is my new friend, Dr. Lucas Forge. Lucas, this is my beautiful wife, Maria."

Wiping her hands on her apron, Maria walked forward, holding out her hand.

Lucas was overcome with her beauty and, without thinking, bent over and kissed the back of her hand. In Spanish he said, "I am enchanted."

Maria blushed and looked at José, who started laughing. José grabbed Lucas by the arm and said with mock menace, "Now, I know I will have to kill you."

Maria punched José in the arm. She was quite strong, and Lucas could tell that she actually hurt José, and probably left a mark. José retreated and said, "Owww. That hurt."

Maria said, "Forgive my husband. He is a jealous man."

Lucas replied, "It is okay. I fully understand."

"Well, I hope you are hungry, because there is no food for José tonight."

Lucas realized that he really liked these people. He thought for a moment that someday, he too would like to find a woman like Maria, and spend the rest of his life with her on some beach.

José motioned to a table in the middle of the open courtyard and said, "Let's go outside and let Maria finish her cooking. Do you want a beer?"

"I would love a beer, thank you."

Lucas sat down on a sturdy wooden chair and looked up into the sky. The clouds were turning pink and orange as the sun set. José came out with two bottles of Corona and a small bowl of sliced limes. Before long, Maria started putting plates on the table and then brought out bowls of grilled shrimp and carne asada. Each time she returned from the kitchen, she brought more food, including homemade tortillas, sliced avocado, several salsas, mangos and papaya.

Lucas ate more that night than he ever remembered eating in one sitting. José kept bringing out more bottles of beer, and soon Lucas' head was swimming. He kept praising Maria's cooking and she kept smiling with her brilliant white teeth.

They talked long into the night. Lucas was surprised to find that they were both well educated and worldly. They loved each other deeply and enjoyed an endearing sense of humor. Fate did not allow them to have any children, but they had many nieces and nephews and doted on them whenever they could.

Lucas noticed that, despite their love and laughter, José had a hidden darkness to him that was not shared by Maria. As the night wore on, and Maria excused herself to go to bed, Lucas and José spoke for another hour about the reasons Lucas was there.

José was enraged about the evil surrounding the drug trade. He believed it was immoral and was incensed that so many young people were attracted to it. He knew that the local authorities were often corrupted by the easy and abundant money that came their way if they cooperated with the cartels.

He had been trying to gain information about the dealings of the cartels and the people involved. He learned that the problem was not just local, but extended through Central America and down to South America. He heard rumors of a secret sect that was developing new, and more addictive drugs. People were afraid to talk about the cartels. Those who did talk, often mysteriously disappeared. There was something sinister and even supernatural going on. He told Lucas that there were whispers of some evil shamanistic organization in Argentina that was growing in power and influence.

Perhaps because of the beer, Lucas told José what happened to him in Argentina.

"You disappeared for six weeks and you remember nothing about what happened?"

"Yes. But the most troubling thing is that I was shot, but now there is no evidence of it. The doctors think I was hallucinating, but I have two friends who say they saw me shot. Then six weeks later, there were no signs of me being shot, no scars."

José leaned forward, "I have heard tales of men being healed by sorcerers. We call then Brujos. Some of them are good and they practice white magic. They sometimes perform miracles. Other Brujos are evil. I think the evil ones may be involved in the drug trade. One time, a very drunk drug boss mentioned a name. I think it was Don Benigno. The man was not easily frightened, but he was terrified of this Benigno."

"Is this Don Benigno here in Mexico?"

"No. No. It sounded like he was living in South America, perhaps Paraguay or Argentina. But he has influence all the way to Mexico. He somehow gets the drugs into your country."

"Can you introduce me to this local drug boss?"

"I am afraid not. He disappeared. I suspect he was murdered for talking too much."

Lucas suddenly felt very tired. "Perhaps we can continue talking in the morning."

"Of course, you must be exhausted after your long flight." Looking at his watch, he said. "It is nine o'clock. I think that it is midnight in Washington. Let me show you to your room."

Lucas passed out in the comfortable bed. He was startled awake at three o'clock from a nightmare. He dreamt that he was trapped in a metal room and could not get out. Men in brown robes were singing in some foreign language and one old man was making him drink some vile liquid. He started to die in his nightmare, and then he woke up. He sat up in bed, drenched in sweat despite the cool air. Lucas tried to forget the nightmare by remembering verses from Epictetus. Soon, he fell asleep again.

He awakened again while it was still dark outside. He knew that it was probably five o'clock, and his watch agreed. He listened carefully, but could hear no sounds, except for a rooster crowing in the distance. Slipping into a pair of shorts, he tiptoed to the center courtyard. Orion was low in the sky. Scorpio was hidden by the rooftop. He powered through his exercises and then sat down on the wooden chair.

He heard some noises from the kitchen and soon he smelled the delicious scent of brewing coffee. In a short time, Maria emerged with a tray and two cups of steaming coffee.

Sitting down next to him, Maria handed him a cup and took one for herself. The sky was beginning to lighten with the coming dawn. She turned to Lucas and said, "You are a curious man. I am afraid your curiosity will cause you great pain someday."

Lucas nodded. "I have been told that, Maria. Thank you for the coffee and for your hospitality. José was correct in saying that you are the best cook south of the Rio Grande. I envy your relationship with him."

Maria chuckled. "There are many good women in the world, Lucas. I think, perhaps, you do not notice them because you are too focused on fighting demons." She looked up at the fading stars.

Lucas marveled at her beauty. She was not a young woman, but her beauty was illuminated from her soul. He could think of no other way to explain it. He had often been seduced by the surface attractiveness of young women, only to be disappointed by their inexperience and shallowness. He wanted more in life, but his chosen profession made it impossible to share his life with another. He knew that it would be unfair for any women to become involved with him. He had trained himself to become oblivious to any flirtatiousness by them.

Maria said, "There is going to be a party tonight. It is an annual festival of sorts. There will be music and dancing and I am cooking some food for it. Perhaps you would like to join us?"

Lucas smiled, "Maria, if you are cooking, there is no way I would miss it."

Hours later, Lucas and José continued their conversation, Maria busied herself in the kitchen and Luca found himself distracted by the delicious aromas of her concoctions. José made a simple lunch of tortillas and carne asada with grilled green onions. Before long, it was time to get ready for the party.

Lucas took a long shower. The water was heated by a large black vessel sitting on top of the roof of the hacienda. The sun heated the water all day and no extra power was needed. He dressed himself and came out to José's living room. Maria took one look at him and said, "Oh no. You cannot wear that outfit for tonight"

Lucas was perplexed and only said, "What?" He was wearing light blue plaid pants and a contrasting chartreuse plaid shirt.

"Oh, Lucas. You are as bad as José. I try to dress him before he leaves the house, but sometimes I am too late. Lucas, you must be color blind, you poor soul."

"Well, I have been told that. What's wrong?"

"Just, well, everything. Where are your clothes? Let me pick out something nice for you."

Lucas took her to his duffle bag and unzipped it. She rummaged around for a few minutes, and selected a pair a khaki pants, a brown belt, and a light blue shirt. "Please, wear these instead."

"Okay, Maria. I trust you."

Maria left the room, shaking her head, saying, "Dios Mio."

The party was on the beach, overlooking the placid Sea of Cortez. There was a live band, energetically playing a series of old standards and more modern music. The band members were dressed identically in garish uniforms, topped by large colorful sombreros.

There were dozens of portable stands, forming a crooked line, selling a variety of foods and desserts. Small families weaved through the large crowd, selling jewelry, scarves, hats, hammocks, and various trinkets. The crowd consisted of people of all age groups and ethnicities, tourists and locals, and they mingled freely amongst each other. The atmosphere was festive and hyperactive. Beer flowed freely from the rear of large trailers and makeshift bars.

Maria and José had their own stand, and the lines were longest in front of them. Maria kept introducing Lucas as her cousin from Arizona, and he gave up trying to remember people's names after the first thirty encounters. That is, until he met Alícia. Maria had a special glow about her when introducing Lucas to Alícia.

He had never been so smitten by a woman. She had long wavy black hair, radiant olive skin, emerald green eyes, and a smile that made his heart stop. She seemed shy outwardly, but he sensed an intrinsically passionate soul. Lucas found himself at an awkward loss for the appropriate words. Fortunately, Maria got the conversation going until Lucas could get his bearings.

Soon, Lucas and Alícia were chatting like old friends. They began walking and before long, they found themselves on a deserted stretch of beach. They removed their shoes and walked in the warm water of the Sea of Cortez. She was a professor of history and archeology at the university. Her father was a renowned archeologist and she followed in his footsteps. Her mother taught languages at the same university. She had been engaged once, but her fiancé was tragically murdered two years ago, as an innocent bystander, caught in the middle of a shoot out between rival cartels.

Alícia grieved deeply since that time but was finally getting back out into the world. She had known José and Maria for many years, both in Mexico City, and now in Puerto Penasco. Maria insisted that she come to the party tonight. Lucas would be forever grateful.

Around midnight, Lucas realized that they were far from the party. He had lost track of the time and direction. He was worried that José and Maria had closed up shop and might be headed home. He shared his worries with Alícia, and she reluctantly agreed that they should start back. The music was still going strong and they followed the faint sounds like a homing beacon. The half moon was high in the sky, and the sand glittered like tiny diamonds under their feet.

Lucas was frustrated that he could not reveal much about his current life. He found himself having to tell white lies about what he really did for a living. Alícia smiled, but he could tell that she didn't fully believe his prevarications. He did not want to lie to her, and felt torn because of his need for deception.

For the first time, he began regretting some of the life choices he had made. He knew he was going to have to leave shortly, if he were to continue on his chosen path. He knew it would not be fair to her to involve her in his life.

The closer they got to rejoining the party, the worse he felt. Alícia noticed the change in him and asked him what was wrong.

"Is it something I said?" she asked, taking his hand.

"Oh no, God no," he replied. "I just have some business to attend to over the next few days, and suddenly, I am not looking forward to it. I have really enjoyed our evening together, and wish that it would never end."

Alícia stopped walking, still holding on to his hand. Feeling the tug, Lucas turned around. Alícia was staring up into his face. Her eyes were glowing like two green pools in the moonlight. Lucas wanted to dive into those pools and never come out.

He pulled her close and leaned down, wanting to press his lips against her lush mouth. He came within inches, when she suddenly stiffened, turned her head, and pulled back.

"Please no. I am sorry, Lucas. It is too soon for me."

Lucas felt his passion drain from his body like a deflating balloon.

Seeing his disappointment, she quickly added, "I like you, Lucas, I really do. It is just that I was not prepared for this evening. I thought I was going to spend a few hours with Maria and then go home. I never anticipated that I would meet someone, especially someone like you."

"That makes two of us. I just came for Maria's cooking. She is a smart and passionate woman. She knows how to satisfy hunger of the stomach, and maybe of the soul. I now believe that she set this whole thing up, you and I."

Alícia nodded. "Yes, I have seen her operate. She takes great pleasure in orchestrating people's movements. There is a Yiddish word for it, shadchanit. In Spanish, we call it casamentera. She is like a matchmaker."

Lucas said, "Normally, I would be resentful for being manipulated so easily. But tonight, I find myself feeling overjoyed. I have not felt like this for a long time, maybe never."

"Yes. I was not sure I could, or should ever feel this way again. We are just talking, but I almost feel like I am betraying Rolando, my fiancé."

They walked in silence for a few minutes. Lucas spotted José's white Ford truck parked next to their stall. José was just finishing loading their stall into the back. The fiesta was still going strong, and the people were talking and singing more loudly. Screams of laughter were coming from all directions.

Lucas started to help José and asked. "You are leaving the Fiesta?"

José replied, "Yes, we ran out of food. There are many more people here this year. We were not expecting such a crowd. Maria is heartbroken. She cannot stand disappointing people."

Lucas saw Maria sitting down in a circle of women. There was a lively discussion going on. Seeing Lucas and Alícia standing near the truck, Maria excused herself and came over to them.

"You two disappeared. I thought we were going to have to send out search party," she said.

Lucas felt his face redden. Maria could see right through him. He thought she could have a stellar career with the agency.

She continued, "So, did you two have a good time? Did you find something to talk about?"

Alícia smiled at her and replied, "You know we did, you little Bruja."

Lucas stiffened at the word. Something was tugging at his mind, but it was just out of reach. He flashed on the memory of sitting under that tree outside Posadas. His head began to hurt.

Looking up into the sky, he found Orion. Scorpio appeared to be getting closer.

Chapter 16   The Ledger

Chapter 17

The Genesis Connection

José found Lucas sitting in the courtyard, sipping coffee. Maria was singing softly in the kitchen. Pulling out a chair, José sat down and began speaking in hushed tones.

"I may have found the man we are looking for. It will not be easy, as we will have to find a way to get him alone, away from his crew. We will need backup."

"I might be able to bring someone down from the agency, but it may take a day or two."

"No. That will not work. We have to move on this tonight. They are going to the Reef bar, and this might be our last opportunity."

Lucas thought a moment, "Do you know anyone reliable?"

"There is a man I have used once or twice. He is ex-military, a former scout/sniper, and he is good in crowds. He is like a chameleon and can blend in anywhere, if he needs to."

"Is he available? I would like to meet him," Lucas said.

"I will check." José walked into the house to make the call. He passed Maria in the kitchen and goosed her on the way. She screamed and threw a hot tortilla at him. José caught it, and waved a thank you. Maria mumbled something under her breath, but she was smiling.

In a few minutes, José returned and sat down again. "I found him, and he is looking forward to it. He says he has been bored with nothing to do lately. He had a good idea. He will bring a female friend, whom we can use as a distraction at the bar."

"Can we meet them this morning?"

"It is already set up. There is a secluded spot near the beach where we can go and not be observed."

Soon, José and Lucas were sitting on the weathered picnic bench, under the meager shade of a scraggly tree. Lucas spotted two figures walking toward them from the distant parking lot. Lucas knew that the pair had multiple possible entry paths to the table, but one of pair likely chose the path that kept the sun at their backs. *Smart move, unless it was unintended.*

Lucas studied the man first. He was trim, almost lanky, and walked with a laconic stride. He was wearing black jeans and a white shirt. A black cowboy hat sat on his head. The woman was short and petite, her long blond hair tied up in a pony tail. She wore a pale blue sun dress and flat sandals. When they got closer, Lucas could see the man's face. His eyes were constantly scanning the surroundings. The man had dark brown eyes, a tanned, crooked nose attached to a rugged and scarred face. His hair was long, hanging past his ears, but it appeared to be combed, and almost styled.

José stood and reached out his hand. The two men shook hands, but the newcomer's eyes never left Lucas' gaze. José turned to Lucas and said, "This is the friend I was telling you about. Lucas, may I introduce Carlos Cholla del Rio. Lucas noticed that the man tensed slightly at the use of his full name. Lucas stood and came around the side of the table to shake the man's hand. His grip was strong, but not crushing, as some macho men did when meeting another. His brown eyes were intelligent and piercing. He obviously was sizing up Lucas, just as Lucas was doing to him.

Carlos turned slightly to the women on his left and spoke in a deep baritone voice, "May I introduce my friend, Marta."

Marta nodded, but did not extend her hand. Her eyes looked at José and Lucas with mild suspicion.

José said, "Please, let us sit down."

The men waited for Marta to be seated first. Lucas watched Carlos make a 360 degree scan of the landscape before sitting down next to her. Lucas had just completed his own 360 degree scan when their eyes met. Carlos had a thin knowing smile on his face. Both men noticed that they each had a concealed weapon stuffed under their shirts.

José spent twenty minutes discussing their target and their plans. Carlos suggested a few changes that made tactical sense. He recommended that they take two vehicles and arrive separately in pairs. He pulled out a piece of paper, and plotted their entry and escape routes, including several alternatives. Lucas appreciated that the man was thorough, considering alternatives for when things did not go as planned, as often they did not.

A few hours after the sun had disappeared behind the Baja Mountains, José and Lucas arrived at the Reef bar. They sat near the entrance, so that they could spot their target coming in. Carlos and Marta would arrive later. The bar was filled, mostly with tourists who were getting happier and louder by the minute. The crowd was young, and the mating rituals were in overdrive. The American music was loud, almost deafening. Lucas knew this was a mixed blessing. It made communication more difficult, but it could also cover up any disturbance they might make.

José nudged Lucas under the table, his eyes signaling the direction. Lucas turned slightly and saw a thirty-something man, dressed in a red silk shirt and tight black dress pants enter the bar. Two large men accompanied him, and it was obvious that they were his bodyguards, and they were not here to party. The target was Latino, but there were traces of Aryan in his blue eyes. His hair was perfectly coiffed. His eyes scanned the room, looking for women, as he ignored the males in the bar.

He ordered something from the bar, and the bartender produced a large margarita, which the target swallowed in three gulps. He ordered another one immediately. The two goons stood close by him, scanning the room with ill- concealed disgust on their faces. They were not drinking. The target flashed a large roll of twenties, looking around as if hoping some women would notice. Finishing the second drink, he ordered a third, tipping the bartender with one of the twenties.

The target tried starting up conversations with several different women, but they quickly gave him the brush off. He had another drink.

Carlos entered the bar wearing the same outfit he had on earlier. Marta sashayed in behind him. She had changed, and was now wearing a skin tight little black dress, with the emphasis on little. Her silky blond hair was down, flowing past her shoulders. She wore black high heels and she knew how to work them. Several men in the bar gave her lustful looks.

Carlos scanned the room and spotted Lucas and José. José used his eyes to point out the target, and Carlos nodded unobtrusively. He and Marta made a wide berth around the bar and walked to the other end. The target ordered another drink, and was getting clumsy in his movements. He leaned up and whispered something into the ear of the taller one of his goons. The large man frowned, and said something to the other goon, who just nodded.

The target and the tall goon began walking toward the rear of the bar, heading to the restroom. Carlos turned and made his way there ahead of them.

Lucas said, "Game time."

They stood up and followed at a distance. Marta moved to the bar in front of the remaining goon. The man's eyes suddenly showed interest. She stumbled slightly and dropped her clutch bag at his feet. As he bent over to pick it up, she swiftly pushed a syringe into his neck. He rose up with a surprised look on his face. His legs started to buckle, and she skillfully eased him onto a bar stool. José made the assist, and turned the man around, facing the bar. José lowered the man's head to the counter. People either didn't notice, or didn't care.

José and Marta quickly exited the bar through the front entrance, José's arm around her waist. Several of the men in the bar stood looking at her departure with crestfallen faces. Lucas continued to the bathroom. Pushing the door open, he spotted Carlos standing in front of a urinal.

The target entered a stall and soon the sounds of retching could be heard. The goon stood facing the closed stall, rocking side by side in nervousness and indecision.

Carlos left the urinal and started passing close by the goon. In a swift movement, he struck the goon's throat and performed a leg sweep, taking the goon to the ground. The man's head hit the tile with a loud crack. He was unconscious without making another sound. The retching continued from inside the stall.

Lucas helped Carlos maneuver the goon into an empty stall and closed the door. Lucas stuffed a small wad of paper towels into the door, wedging it shut. The retching had stopped and the target came out of the stall, looking green. His eyes widened when he noticed that his goon was gone. Carlos spun him around and placed a choke hold around the man's neck. The target passed out in seconds.

Holding the unconscious man between them, they left the bathroom, and made their way to the rear exit. Several customers stared at them, but then shook their heads, probably thinking that the man had too much to drink and had passed out. A few gave Lucas a sympathetic look.

They exited the rear patio and pushed the target into the back seat of the waiting vehicle. Marta was driving. Carlos followed the man into the back seat and closed the door. Marta pulled out, and José pulled up into the now vacant spot. Lucas climbed in and they followed Marta.

The two vehicles pulled up to an old abandoned warehouse on the outskirts of the city, near the air strip. Carlos and Lucas dragged the now bound and gagged target inside the building. He was struggling against his bonds and muffled screaming leaked out from behind his gag. They sat him down on a metal chair that was welded to the floor. Marta drove off with a roll of twenties in her clutch bag, and a smile on her face.

Carlos slapped the target. The man was terrified, and the front of his pants became shiny with his own urine.

Lucas pulled up a chair and began the interrogation. He was finished in less than twenty minutes. No torture was needed. The man had given up all he knew, and had even revealed information that he did not know he knew. Carlos then blindfolded the man and drove him ten miles to a remote desert location. He removed the blindfold, untied him, and let him go, with only a bottle of water. Carlos then drove back to the warehouse.

Lucas and José were engaged in an intense conversation. When Carlos arrived, José filled him in on the details. Their target had flown in from Mendoza Argentina to cement relationships with cartel associates throughout Mexico. He was an upper level manager in the Mendoza Cartel, having advanced only because his father was a lawyer, near the top of the management structure.

José said, "The guy was obviously weak, and in over his head. He likely would already be dead, if not for his father's influence. Lucas pulled some mental judo on the guy. He gave up the names of cartel members in four different countries."

"Four countries? The organization is that big?" Carlos asked.

José continued, "It is getting bigger. He told Lucas that there had been a bloody coup in the last few months, and a new leader had emerged out of the carnage. His name is Don Benigno."

Lucas added, "It sounds like everyone in the organization is terrified of this Benigno, not only because of his ruthlessness, but because supposedly, he is some kind of shaman. They say he has weird powers over others. There are rumors that he can kill a man using only his eyes. He has a group of followers or acolytes, and they too, supposedly possess unnatural powers."

"Come on, you don't really believe that crap. Do you?" Carlos asked.

"It doesn't matter what I believe. It matters that this guy believes it, and he thinks that many in the cartels believe it. But, that is not all."

"Of course not. Okay, I'll bite." Carlos said. He had a cynical look on his face.

Lucas added, "The worst part is that Don Benigno has started a new ambitious project. He has hundreds of chemists who are working around the clock, developing new, more powerful drugs. They are trying to create a new class of drug addicts with some new drug. Apparently, anyone can be fully addicted after just one dose."

"One dose addiction. That is going to create havoc." Carlos said.

Lucas added, "Supposedly it comes in pill and liquid form, and is tasteless and odorless. Theoretically, it could be released into the water supply."

Carlos looked at José. "Something tells me that this project thing gets worse."

José said, "He said that some other new drugs have been developed that can kill anyone who gets in their way. Our little friend said that these new drugs were untraceable in the body."

Carlos said, "Great. Is there a name for this project?"

Lucas answered, "He called it the Genesis Project."

Lucas thought back to Posadas. Jake said their mission was called Operation Genesis. Lucas did not believe in coincidences. *Did the Director know about the Genesis project? If so, why did he not tell us?* He noticed that Carlos was looking at him questioningly.

Carlos asked, "The Genesis Project, what does that mean?"

Lucas thought for a few moments before answering. "I do not know. I can only hypothesize. Benigno sounds like a very intelligent and resourceful man who also may be delusional. He may think he is God. According to our target, Benigno plans to use these various drugs to take over South America, then North America, and then the world, with him as God. If we do not find a way to stop him, he just might succeed."

Acknowledgments

A book can be a labor of love, sweat, long nights, and early mornings. Family and friends are often ignored during the process of creation. As a writer, there were times when I was physically with others, but my mind was elsewhere, involved with the cast of characters, plot lines, details, and sudden insights. Please know that I love you and care about you, my family and friends, and I am blessed to have you in my life despite my failings.

This was my second full novel of fiction. I ran into many dead ends and painted myself into seemingly inextricable corners, only to find that my subconscious mind would be working behind the scenes, coming up with solutions.

First, and foremost, I thank my wife, the fascinating, fetching and exuberant Susan. You put up with too much loneliness during my affair with this book. Still, you continued to support me with your passion and insight. Thank you for making me take long walks in the mornings and reminding me of our love.

I thank my long-time friend and fellow adventurer, Brad Lindsay, trike pilot, inventor, creative thinker, and lover of fun and excitement. Your passion for Mexico and Pinacate, helped inspire me in so many ways. Click here to check out his energy saving products.

Not least of all, I thank my loving daughter, Hallory, whose transformation into an intelligent, creative, and beautiful young woman, has opened my eyes to the world of a new generation.

I wish to thank and acknowledge Front Sight Firearms Training Institute for teaching me the comfort and skill at arms, and for helping protect the Constitution of the United States.

I also thank Dennis Prager, and Prager University, for the wonderful videos he provides on a wide variety of important topics. Hillsdale College has also been an inspiration with their free courses on the US Constitution and the many transcribed speeches provided in their free publication, Imprimus.

To my many mentors and friends throughout the years who have blessed me with your knowledge, insight, and support. Some of you know who you are, and some will remain anonymous for varied reasons. Thank you all.

Finally, I wish to thank you, my readers. I hope you enjoyed reading this series as much as I have enjoyed writing them. If you like these books, please tell your friends.

Here is a sample of Book One in the Lucas Forge series, The Mendoza Connection. Please buy this book to continue the adventure.

The Mendoza Connection in Paperback or Kindle.
http://goo.gl/B8vvWl

The Mendoza Connection

A Lucas Forge Novel
By Scott Sindelar

PUBLISHED BY:
Clean House Press
ISBN 978-1-888774-06-1

Chapter 1   Monday. Lucas Forge- The Call- Arizona

Dr. Lucas Forge was startled awake, the images of his dream ripped away by the insistent ring tone from his cell phone. The room was still dark, vaguely lit by the green LEDs of his alarm clock. Turning his head and blinking his pale blue eyes into focus, he read the dial; 4:07 AM. His phone rang again, triggering a flood of thoughts as his brilliant mind scanned through the possibilities of who would be calling, and why.

Raising his head, he quickly scanned the room. Seeing no movement and nothing out of place, he reached over and tugged at the thin sheet covering his naked body. He slid his muscular legs onto the soft carpet on the floor. He stood up, gaining his balance, and grabbed his phone on top of the rich walnut dresser. Scanning the screen, he saw the foreign area code and the image of a tanned and weathered man wearing a black cowboy hat, and jagged snowcapped mountains in the background. The man in the image was smiling with a full set of brilliant white teeth, but his dark eyes told a different story.

Forge took a deep breath and felt the hairs on the back of his neck stand to attention. Using his index finger, he activated his phone and raised it to his ear, simultaneously scanning the room once more for good measure. With an odd mixture of happiness and dread, he spoke into the phone.

THE MENDOZA CONNECTION

"Buenos fucking dias, Carlos. Christ, it is 4 AM!"

Forge listened to a few moments of whooshing and static before his old friend Carlos replied.

Speaking with impeccable English, and without a trace of Spanish accent, Carlos retorted, "Well, it's 8 o'clock here in Mendoza, and it's sunny and warm already."

Forge responded with feigned irritation, "Yeah, how nice for you. It's still dark here in Arizona, cabrón."

Forge had heard a rooster crowing in the background behind Carlos' deep baritone voice. His memory brought up an image of the beautiful city of Mendoza. He remembered the miles of wide sidewalks filled with tables and chairs and people walking or sitting, drinking rich Argentine coffee. He flashed on a memory of sitting at one of those tables, staring into the deep green eyes of a black haired woman, Alícia. A pang of regret tugged at his heart. His memory was interrupted by Carlos' voice.

"Okay, Lucas. I know what you're thinking, Vato. You're thinking of her, Alícia. I'm sorry, my friend. You never listen to me. You've got to let her go. She's gone and I cannot find her."

"I know. I know," Lucas growled slowly, shaking his head. "Listen, amigo, I'm standing here naked, and it's still 4 AM."

"Ayi, Vato. I love you, hombre, but I don't need that image in my head."

Carlos pushed forward from his leaning position against his old olive drab Land Cruiser. He absently brushed the reddish dust from the back of his jeans. His dark brown eyes focused on the mountains in the distance, to clear his mind of the image of a naked Lucas. He watched a hawk slowly circling in an early morning thermal. The hawk's wingtips were splayed open for maximum lift.

Carlos inhaled deeply through his tanned and crooked nose. The fragrant and warm moist air of the Argentine Pampas filled his lungs.

"Lucas," Carlos started slowly, trying to formulate the best way to begin. "There is something down here that you will want to see."

Lucas stared at the wall in front of him. The white paint was glowing a faint green from the alarm clock to his left. His eyes narrowed. He could not help himself, as his trained mind automatically analyzed the tone in Carlos' voice. There was something he heard in his friend's voice: darkness; and beneath the surface, a little fear. Lucas was suddenly fully awake. In the thirty years of their friendship, he had never heard fear in Carlos' voice. Darkness, yes; but not fear. It was neither in his nature, nor in his breeding.

"You still there, Lucas?" Carlos asked, a little softer now.

"I'm here," Lucas replied evenly. "When should I come?"

Carlos looked up at the circling hawk. The thermal was carrying it gently downwind. Carlos felt a fleeting twinge of envy, not only of the hawk's ability to fly, but of its freedom. He answered Lucas's question.

"Yesterday would be fine."

There it was again; Lucas sensed the fear in Carlos' tone. He looked again at the image of Carlos on his phone. The stomach tightened. He thought for a moment about all of the appointments he would have to cancel, but only for a moment. He raised the phone back to his ear.

"I will get started immediately. Buenos Aires or Mendoza?"

The two cities were 1200 kilometers apart. Lucas remembered it was 12 hours by car along the two-lane Nacional Ruta 7, or less than two hours by air. Lucas did not relish a 12 hour, white-knuckle drive with Carlos behind the wheel. If they drove, they would probably make the trip in less than 10 hours, assuming they survived Carlos' maniacal driving.

Carlos thought for a few moments, "Mendoza would be better. I am just outside the city, and I will need to get supplies and find some, uh, cosas especiales. It may take a few days."

Lucas nodded understandingly for both of them, and thought, *cosas especiales, special items, indeed.*

"All right, my friend. I'll text you my itinerary and call you before the final flight to Mendoza from Santiago. I'll see you in a few days."

Carlos whispered, "Vaya con Dios, amigo. Vaya con Dios."

Carlos ended the call and looked up once more for the hawk. It was a tiny speck headed east. Out of habit, a habit that always served him well during his years of military service, he slowly turned around, his eyes scanning the horizon a full 360°. The long mountain chain of the Andes was to the west. The Pampas spread out to the south and to the east. To the north, far behind his Land Cruiser, was a small ranchero in the distance. A wisp of smoke rose from the chimney of the adobe walled hacienda. He stared at the small structure and its cluster of outbuildings for a good minute. Seeing no movement, he walked back to his truck.

Standing next to his truck, he removed a piece of old dried paper from his shirt pocket. Once again, the drawings on the paper puzzled him. Surely it was a map, but what did the symbols mean? Carlos had heard rumors that the local crime syndicate, the one he called the Mendoza Mafia, had been taken over by some mysterious man with mysterious ways. He was supposedly some kind of sorcerer, a Brujo Negro, and he was wealthy and ruthless. He had assassinated many of the mafia Dons and was now also in control of the manufacture and distribution of new, powerful drugs.

Carlos tried to research the Brujos Negros but could find very little information. He stumbled upon the map in the city library in Barioloche, in a collection of old books. He found it in a book about the Brujos. Trying to make a connection between the ancient Brujos and the modern drug trade proved frustrating. When he questioned some of the street drug dealers, he sometimes heard the name Don Benigno. The men he questioned seemed terrified to even mention that name. *The map must be the key. Lucas might be able to figure it out.*

Carlos' black cotton shirt was becoming even blacker down his back and under his armpits, wet from his sweat. His black cowboy boots were sprinkled with the red dust. Carlos looked thin and wiry, his incredible strength and stamina hidden by the loose cotton shirt and denim jeans. His lanky shape and black cowboy hat made him look taller than he really was.

His rugged and scarred face, and that thousand yard stare, stopped many barroom fights without his having to raise a fist. Patrons often bought him a drink, as offerings of appeasement. His bright toothy smile and quick wit attracted many a señorita, and left behind many broken hearts.

He was partial to the petite natural blonde and blue-eyed Argentine ladies so common in Mendoza, in Barioloche and in parts of Buenos Aires. They could trace their ancestries back to northern Europe when their ancestors fled the war-torn countries during and between the two world wars. Carlos was still amused to hear the musical Argentine Spanish emerge from their pouty Aryan lips. They seemed to swoon at the contrast of his dark muscular skin against their pale flesh.

As Carlos climbed easily into his Land Cruiser, he heard a rooster crow in the distance. It crowed three times.

About the Author
Scott Sindelar, Ph.D.

Photo Credit: Susan Carroll Sindelar

Forensic Psychologist, author, adventurer, mountaineer, and Trike pilot. Dr. Scott Sindelar has published a series of Lucas Forge Action/Adventure/Sci-Fi novels including: The Mendoza Connection, The Genesis Connection, The Pinacate Connection, and now the exciting The Brujo Connection.
He is also the author of the non-fiction self-help book: Conquering the Fear of Rejection; a Children's book: The Adventures of Ralph-The Superhero Flying

Squirrel, and a short story: The Man Who Would Be Savior

Special Offer

Get a Free Short Story

The Man Who Would Be Savior

Go to

ScottSindelarBooks.com